PLEASE DISAPPEAR

THE ARUN SHAH MYSTERY SERIES

PLEASE DISAPPEAR: An unputdownable thriller with a dark twist
(Book 1)

BLACK DOT, RED WATER (Book 2)

PLEASE DISAPPEAR

The Arun Shah Mysteries Book 1

M.K. Shivakoti

LakePoint Media

Chicago

M.K. Shivakoti
Visit author's website at www.mkshivakoti.com

ISBN-13: 978-0-692-11481-0
ISBN-10: 0-692-11481-5

For my son, Etash.

CONTENTS

M.K. Shivakoti

PROLOGUE

Ten years ago

Clair's hands were covered in flour. Tomorrow was Ethan's thirteenth birthday and she was baking a vanilla cake with chocolate filling, his favorite. He had been a little off this morning. "Bad dream, Ma," he had said. *I hope he feels better after seeing the cake,* she thought.

The doorbell chimed.

Clair looked at the kitchen clock. 1:28 PM. She wasn't expecting anyone. Ethan wouldn't be home from school for another two hours and Nick not until late that evening.

The doorbell chimed again . . . and again.

"I'm coming," she shouted while washing her hands. She wiped them on a paper towel, walked toward the entrance, and opened the door.

The cheerfulness on her face dropped instantly, replaced by colorless horror.

Outside, Ethan's white shirt was tucked out, yellow-brown patches all over it. His usually well-combed hair roughed up. His left eye swollen.

"What happened?" Clair cried as she reached for him.

But before she could touch him, he swiftly raised his left hand and slapped his swollen eye with great force. "Repent," he said. "Repent . . . Repent."

Clair's hand stopped midair, her body leaning back involuntarily in utter disbelief.

"Ethan!" she exclaimed and held him tight in her arms, her heart wanting to jump out of her chest. Her eyes were already welling up.

"Repent . . . Repent . . . Repent . . ."

"Sshh . . ." Clair put her arm around his shoulder, took him into the living room, put him on a couch, and kissed him on his forehead.

Oh my god, oh my god!

She held his hands and buried her face in his palms.

"Please tell me, honey, what happened?" she begged as tears rolled down her cheeks.

"Gabriel, Ma . . ." Ethan said.

Clair wiped her tears and looked at Ethan in disbelief.

"The blind kid? He did this to you?"

Ethan didn't say anything.

"Talk to me, honey, did Gabriel do this to you? She hesitated.

"I need to repent, Ma . . ."

Clair felt a twitch in Ethan's left arm. She held his hand tightly.

Should I call the doctor? No, I'll call Nick. He'll know what to do.

"I dreamt last night. I must repent. I didn't tell you this, but I bullied Gabriel. I won't go near him again. I need to repent . . . repent . . . repent."

"Sshh! I will call Daddy home and it will all be fine, okay, honey? No one needs to repent." Clair's voice trembled. She put Ethan's hands inside his pockets and laid him on the couch, his head resting on the armrest. Her shoes clacked loudly on the hardwood floor as she rushed to the kitchen.

Gabriel? Oh my God, is he not blind?

She grabbed her cell phone from the kitchen counter and dialed Nick. The phone rang once . . . twice . . .

Pick it up, Nick! Please pick it up.

"Ello!" Nick said cheerfully on the other end of the line.

"Nick! Oh, Nick! Ethan . . . Ethan . . . You need to come home . . ." Clair burst into tears.

THUD! THUD!

Clair looked into the living room.

"ETHAN!" she screamed.

Her phone dropped to the floor as she covered her mouth with both hands. Nick's concerned voice only faintly heard.

"Honey, Hello! What's going on . . . Hon . . ."

Ethan had climbed off the couch and was sitting on the floor on his knees, legs together, his butt on his heels. His hands still in his pockets. He bent his spine forward and with all his might hit his head on the hardwood floor.

THUD!

He drew his body back, bent forward, and hit the floor again, and again, and again . . .

THUD! THUD! THUD!

No more a mumble, he now screamed,

"REPENT . . . REPENT . . . REPENT . . ."

M.K. Shivakoti

PART ONE

ONE

August 2016

The red light turned green and an electric-blue Harley Softail took a right turn. After less than fifty yards, it swerved right again and entered the parking lot of the Worcester Police Department. The driver was decked out all in black. Backpack, boots, leather pants, leather jacket, and a helmet with a tinted visor. The motorcycle came to a stop. The driver pushed the kickstand to the ground, slightly tilting the bike into park.

Sandra climbed off and removed her helmet. Half of her jet-black hair flowed down to her right shoulder. The other side of her part was undercut very short.

She unlocked the hinged clasp under the seat, hung the helmet by its strap, and relocked it securely. She adjusted her in-ear headphone and turned the volume up. Deep Purple screamed . . . *and fire in the sky.* She grabbed a coffee mug from the bike's cup holder and walked toward the front door of the building.

Inside her office, Sandra put the coffee mug on her desk, tossed her backpack on a chair, and booted up her desktop. She looked at the manila envelope the receptionist had handed her as she entered the building.

The sticky note on the envelope read:

> *Sandy,*
> *I need you on this. Could you please take a look?*
> *Jim.*

She plopped into her chair and dropped the contents of the envelope on her desk. A file folder labeled *Case Notes: Sara Sardana* and two CDs labeled *Sara Sardana: Amigo's Mexican Grill* and *Sara Sardana: Charming Lady* sprawled on the desk.

She skimmed through the case notes and considered the key points.

> *Sara Sardana worked at the Charming Lady store located at the Greenmile Shopping Center.*
> *On July 31ˢᵗ, at 3:11 PM, she signed out from the store.*
> *Ordered a Ride-O-Share.*
> *Never arrived home.*
> *Boyfriend filed missing person report the next day.*

Sandra looked at the bottom right corner of her monitor.

> *8:31 AM*
> *August 3*

She took out the CD labeled *Sara Sardana: Amigo's Mexican Grill* from its sleeve and put it in the DVD reader on her computer. Seconds later, Windows Media Player auto-played the content.

The CCTV footage was in color. The top half of the video showed a store. The name of the store wasn't visible, but the window was decorated with handbags and mannequins wearing women's clothing. Just below the store was the sidewalk where people were walking.

Sandra scanned the video to a little past 3 PM and hit *play*. As women came out and went inside the store, Sandra compared them with Sara's photo on her desk.

At 3:17 *PM*, a young woman walked out. Sandra thought she looked very much like Sara. The woman walked across the street and pulled the glass door below the CCTV camera and went inside, out of view of the camera. She came out after fifteen minutes and stood on the sidewalk, facing away from the camera. After several minutes, she pulled her jacket closer to her chest and walked to the left side of the video. Her head was turning slightly left when she vanished beyond the camera's field of view.

Hmm . . .

Sandra rewound the video and watched it again.

Trying to look behind you, Sara?

She watched the video a couple more times.

She took the CD out of the DVD player and put in the other CD, *Sara Sardana: Charming Lady.*

Like before, the video auto-played. On the top half of the screen was a different store. The window of this store was decorated with a poster of a burrito, devil-horned with two green peppers.

Sandra was looking for the same woman she had seen in Amigo's CCTV footage, when she noticed a tall figure in her periphery leaning on the doorjamb to her office.

She looked up toward the door, her hand hovering over the mouse.

"I appreciate this, Sandy," Jim said, wiping his nose with a brown paper towel.

"God! What's wrong with your face?" Sandra said.

Jim's nose was red, his eyes watery, and his skin yellow. He continuously wiped his nose with the paper towel while finger-combing his gray-black hair with his other hand.

"I think my allergies are running wild," Jim said.

"Looks like more than just allergies to me. Did you take something for that?"

"I did but it's not working," Jim said. "That's why I pulled you into this. I need to go see a doctor and figure it out. If it's more serious then I may be out for a couple of days. I'm meeting with the Chief soon to discuss coverage. I'll be only a phone call away, but this needs to continue," he said, pointing at the manila envelope on Sandra's desk. "Already three days since, you know."

Sandra nodded.

"Care to join me to the Chief's?" Jim said.

Sandra shook her head. *No thanks!*

Sandra looked at her monitor, only now realizing that she had forgotten to pause the video.

She's pulling the door . . . now inside Amigo's . . .

"Is that the CCTV footage?" Jim asked as he stepped inside Sandra's office.

Sandra nodded. "I already watched the one from the burrito joint. This one looks like it was filmed from across the street, from the store Sara worked at. I was only getting started."

"Anything interesting?"

Sandra shrugged. "I'll have to ask the boyfriend to confirm, but I may have identified her in the video. Anyway, I was jotting down timelines and things like that. But nothing has jumped out yet."

Were you trying to look behind you, Sara?

"I'm glad you're looking at it. I didn't get a chance yet. That reminds me . . ." Jim put his hand inside his pocket and took out his phone. "Can you follow up on this guy . . . umm, let's see . . ." He jabbed his finger on the phone screen a few times and read, "Chuck Lagano."

Sandra scribbled on her notepad and raised her eyebrows at Jim.

"I had someone speak to Sara's colleagues. You know, from the store."

Sandra nodded.

"They all seem to remember this guy who was in the store on July 31st right around the time Sara was leaving. They said it wasn't unusual for a guy to be in the store, but definitely unusual for him to be in a changing room. You know, since this is a women's apparel store."

I don't think I saw a guy come out from the store.

Sandra nodded again.

"Apparently he was inside the changing room for a long time. When one of the employees knocked to see if everything was all right, he came out holding three bikinis."

Sandra looked at the case notes and then back at Jim.

"I didn't see his name in here," she said, pointing at the file folder.

"Fresh from the oven, Sandy. Sara's coworkers were interviewed last night. I found out this morning too." Jim grinned.

Sandra considered this for a moment.

"Maybe he liked dressing up. Not a crime to check out a bikini." Sandra shrugged.

Jim shook his head. "Not *a* bikini. Three. All different sizes too."

A little weird. But still not a crime.

Sandra didn't say anything.

Jim continued, "Okay, how about this? He went inside the changing room without anything in his hands—one of the employees confirmed this—but he came out holding three bathing suits. Where did he get them, Sandy?"

"They were already inside the changing room," Sandra said nonchalantly.

"Exactly! He picked up bathing suits that other women had tried on and left in the room, after spending fifteen minutes inside the changing room. We know what that means."

Sandra furrowed her eyebrows. "Do we?" she asked.

"What?" Jim said.

"You said, 'We know what that means.' I'm not sure we do."

Jim looked flushed as he ran the paper towel across his nose again. "C'mon, Sandy . . . I guess . . . I guess we don't know exactly, but we can imagine. Besides, my point is that he is a creep, all right!"

A half-smile glazed over Sandra's face. Jim averted his eyes.

Oh, Jim . . .

"Anyway, after the creep paid for the bikinis, he was seen pulling Sara to the side and talking to her. She clocked out right after that so her colleagues didn't get a chance to talk to her."

I didn't see anyone with the woman in the video.

"Did they say she left the store with him?" Sandra asked.

"I don't think so, they said he might have left through the back door to the parking lot, but we will need to verify."

Ah! That's why.

Sandra nodded. "Okay. I'll talk to her colleagues again as well as to the creep," she said and looked at the monitor.

Let's see. Out of the burrito joint, standing on the sidewalk . . .

There was a brief silence.

Jim continued, "I also need to send someone to check out her other job . . ."

Sandra looked up.

"Until recently she seemed to have two jobs. Maybe we'll find something there. But at this time, this Lagano guy is our best bet. Other interviews and public appeals haven't produced anything either."

Sandra nodded.

"Well . . . if you're not coming, I have to go see the Chief. Thanks again, Sandy."

Good luck with the boss man!

As Jim turned and left, Sandra went back to looking at the footage from Charming Lady.

The woman could be seen for a little longer in this footage than in Amigo's. She pulled her jacket closer to her chest as she walked to the right side of the screen. Her brown handbag rocked slightly in the air. She briefly glanced back over her shoulder.

Gotcha! So, you did look back.

Sandra jumped closer, head cocked, nose almost touching the monitor. She couldn't see her expression, but the woman was picking up her pace now.

Sandra scanned the video a few seconds back and played it again. And again. And again.

All right then. You saw someone. That creep? But the backside of the store is on the opposite side . . . maybe I need to look at footage from other stores too. Who else? The boyfriend? Someone from the other job? But certainly someone you wanted to avoid . . .

After several rewinds, Sandra let the video play out. The woman finally disappeared on the right side of the screen. Sandra looked at the time. 3:39 PM.

She rewound the video one more time and hit *pause.*

The woman was completely still, glancing back over her shoulder, facing away from the camera.

Sandra slowly leaned back on her chair, clasped her hands behind her head, and stared pensively at the screen.

Who spooked you, Sara?

TWO

November 2016

G abriel woke up with a bad headache, his hair and shirt drenched in sweat. Everything in his life was blurry, even in his dreams, but today he wished he couldn't see anything, not even a blur. He quickly rubbed his eyes and looked around. Katie was no more, and this wasn't a dream. He was in his room, *thank God.*

Katie had been showing up in his dreams every night, but never like this. That was the worst nightmare. He was glad it was over.

What about tonight though? Will she come again?

He quivered at the thought and quickly jumped out of bed. An acrid odor emerged from under the covers. He opened the door and ran down the narrow hallway outside.

He did not care today, there was no time for his white cane. His muscle memory would have to work. His room was the last room in the hallway. He ran past the first door on the left. It used to be his mother's room. Gamma kept it locked. She told him they used it for storage now, mostly for Pa's junk.

Across from his mother's room was Gamma's room. But he knew she wouldn't be there this morning; she had a night shift at the hospital. Next, he passed their eat-in-kitchen. It didn't have a door, just an opening with an arch. He almost banged his head on the column supporting the arch but managed to avoid it at the last minute. He took a sharp right and continued running down the hallway toward the door in front of him. He banged on the door with urgency as the apparition from his nightmare started screaming inside his head,

DON'T YOU WANT TO FUCK ME, YOU PRICK? FUCK ME! HERE, FUCK ME!

"Pa, open the door," Gabriel pleaded. "I don't want to sleep. I don't want to dream again. Open the door . . . Pleee . . . Pleeease!" Tears rolled down his cheeks.

FUCK ME! LOOK, FUCK ME!

By the time Pa opened the door, Gabriel was on the floor, sprawled, shaking severely.

THREE

April 2016

Good evening! Welcome to the Marriott!" a blond woman greeted from behind the front desk.

"Hi, I am here to meet with Mr. Roman Bland," said Sara, quickly trying to compose her nerves. She had been anxious all day after running into Mr. Bland that morning at the company diversity event. In a burst of confidence, she had asked if she could meet with him briefly to get guidance regarding her career path. Mr. Bland had said he would be more than happy to meet but he was only available in the evening.

"Later this evening works for me," Sara had replied hastily, unable to hide her excitement.

"Okay. Come by around seven at the Marriott and ask for me at reception. Okay?" he had said.

"Do you have an appointment?" the receptionist asked.

Sara nodded. "Yes, at 7 PM"

"And your name is?"

"Sara Sardana."

The receptionist tapped a few keys on the keyboard and then looked up with a frown. "I don't see any appointments for you. Mr. Bland doesn't seem to have anything on his calendar until 9 AM tomorrow morning."

Sara knitted her brows and bit her lower lip. "Well, see, we made the appointment only a few hours ago," she explained, trying not to speak too quickly, "so it's possible Mr. Bland may not have had time to ask anyone to add it to the calendar yet."

After a brief pause, Sara continued, "He is staying here, isn't he?"

The receptionist nodded.

"Maybe you could call him and ask?"

"Ok. I will call him. Please have a seat." The receptionist pointed to the lobby.

Sara thanked the receptionist, turned around, walked over and sat on a red armchair, facing away from the front desk. She twisted her upper body and turned around to look at the front desk again. The receptionist was on the phone and was looking at the computer. Sara could only see her lips moving; she couldn't hear the conversation. *Was Mr. Bland on the other end of the line?* Her heart raced at the thought. She was going to meet one-on-one with the chairman and the founder of the Bland Corporation. This could change everything.

Don't screw this up, Sara! she thought, only half-aware she was tapping the heel of one of her black pumps nervously on the floor.

Sara was a junior project manager at one of the city's leading IT contractors. The Bland Corporation was her client. It was a job with many possibilities and only one downside—the role was tied to a project. She would have a job for only as long as the project lasted. Most took one year to complete; after that she would have to apply for another project, and then get lucky enough to land it. What bothered her about this arrangement more than anything was the job security—or the lack thereof.

To counter the uncertainty of her contract job, Sara also worked as a part-time sales associate at the Charming Lady store. But managing two jobs was becoming very hard. She got weekends off at the Bland Corporation but not at the retail store. There were many weeks when she was working seven long days.

Sara looked behind her again. The receptionist was still on the phone.

Oh God! Had he not meant it when he invited her to the hotel? How embarrassing it would be if he was just being polite, and she'd changed her clothes and come all the way here only to be turned away. *But why make an appointment if you don't mean it?*

She drew a deep breath and exhaled slowly. *No need to get worked up.* She would meet with him if it were meant to be. If not, oh well! She went back to reminding herself why she was here.

She had thought for a long while about quitting her consulting job and working for the Bland Corporation directly, but the consultant-client agreement had stipulated that the Bland Corporation could only hire a former consultant after two years had passed. She couldn't afford to not work for two years, but if she were able to persuade Mr. Bland to make an exception, it was possible she wouldn't have to. There may have been another option that didn't require her to quit her job. She would tell him her story; the rest was up to him.

A touch on her right shoulder made her jump.

"I am sorry, Ms. Sardana. I didn't mean to startle you, but Mr. Bland is ready for you in his suite. He is sorry about the delay, he was finishing up his dinner," the receptionist said.

Sara stood up, smoothed her skirt, held her leather portfolio case in her left hand, and pulled her hand closer to her chest.

"Which way is it?" Sara asked.

"His suite is on the fourth floor, suite 402. Elevator is over there." The receptionist pointed to the left corner.

"Thank you," said Sara with a smile.

Sara walked up to the elevator landing and pressed the up button. Soon she heard a chime. Above the elevator header, green arrows pointed up. The door opened, revealing interior panels completely walled with mirrors. She pressed the button labeled number four. As the elevator door closed, she turned around to face the back panel and looked at herself in the mirror. She tugged her grey skirt, brushed the lapels of her matching jacket with her palms, and pushed her glasses up onto the bridge of her nose. She caught a few strands of untamed hair and guided them back behind her ear.

Satisfied, she turned around and faced the elevator door. She looked at the floor indicator from the corner of her eyes. It read "2." She turned and looked at the mirror on the left side panel. Two mirrors on the opposite sides of the elevator wall had created infinite Saras. Sara everywhere. Sara finally making it. No more paycheck to paycheck life. Her eyes welled up.

Hold it together Sara!

DON'T SCREW THIS UP!

Her parents had immigrated from India twenty-one years ago, a year before she was born, and worked as grocery store clerks throughout her childhood. They'd made just enough money for the three of them. Sara couldn't deny she'd had a happy childhood and her parents had loved her dearly, but whenever she thought about her childhood, money—or the lack thereof—always bubbled up from her memory.

Her musings were interrupted by a chime. She looked up at the floor indicator. It read, "3."

As the elevator kept moving up, her mind slipped back down memory lane.

After high school, she'd enrolled in college and majored in early elementary education. Soon she'd realized that her fondness for kids didn't translate into fondness for teaching. Not to mention the pay for a career in early elementary education wouldn't be great. Ultimately, it was a Myers-Briggs personality test that had sealed the deal for Sara. She was an ESTJ, "The Executive," clearly not "The Teacher." So, she'd changed her major to business and completed her associate's degree in less than two years. At the age of twenty, when her peers were merely dreaming of spring break vacations, she was already a corporate citizen.

A chime announced that the elevator was approaching the fourth floor. The door opened, and Sara noticed suite 402 immediately to the right. She glanced at her infinite self one more time, drew a deep breath, smiled, and stepped out. Infinity collapsed into one.

FOUR

The door to the suite opened and a bald man with an average build emerged from inside. Mr. Bland was still wearing the same navy-blue pinstripe suit he'd been wearing earlier at the company event. He welcomed her inside his suite and offered her a seat in the living area. A butler was still in the room gathering empty dishes. After the butler left the suite, Mr. Bland asked what she would like to drink. Sara said just water would be fine.

Mr. Bland disappeared into the kitchenette and came back with a spirit glass in one hand and a brandy snifter in the other. Rich golden-brown liquid danced slowly inside the snifter.

"I hope you don't mind if I drink, Sara. It has been a long day."

"Oh, no sir, that is fine,"

"Would you like anything else to drink besides water? I want you to feel comfortable. Don't feel shy to ask," said Mr. Bland and gave the spirit glass to Sara.

"Maybe later, water is fine for now. Thank you," Sara replied. The water was fizzy. *Flavored sparkling water?*

Mr. Bland was looking at her with questioning eyes. *Sparkling water will do,* she thought.

"So? How can I help you, Ms. Sardana?" inquired Mr. Bland.

Sara took a deep breath and explained everything.

Mr. Bland listened thoughtfully. When Sara was done speaking, he remained quiet, looking at Sara with his head tilted slightly to the left, his right index finger on his lips and his thumb under his chin.

"When you applied for the role," Mr. Bland asked, "did you know that the position was temporary, and nothing was guaranteed beyond the contract period?"

"I did know, sir, but I had no choice other than to accept the offer," she replied. "I love my job and am hoping that I can continue to work for the Bland Corporation beyond my contract period, if there are such opportunities available."

Mr. Bland thought for a while, keeping his right index finger and thumb in the same position as before and his right leg crossed over his left. He closed his eyes, tilted his head back, and moved his right hand from his lips to his bearded chin and then to his neck. He softly scratched his neck and then suddenly sat upright, opened his eyes, and looked at Sara. "Well, there is one path available to contract workers that would allow you to seek full-time employment without having to quit your job with the consulting company and wait two years. After your five years of service in a temporary capacity, you become eligible to apply for a few full-time positions."

There was a brief silence and then Sara spoke.

"I am worried about next year, sir. Five years is hard to imagine in the current employment climate. There may not be another lucky opening available to me next year."

"Oh, please don't call me sir."

"Sorry," she said quickly.

He waved off her apology with his hand. "That is okay!"

"Is there a way my case can be reviewed sooner?" Sara asked.

Mr. Bland's expression turned grim.

"I didn't mean . . . I am sorry, my intention was not to . . ." Sara couldn't meet Mr. Bland's eyes and lowered her gaze. Mr. Bland took notice.

"You really want this, don't you, Ms. Sardana?"

"Yes, sir . . . Mr. Bland."

"Well, exceptions can be made, I suppose. After all, others didn't come to me. You did."

Sara looked up and saw a slight smile on Mr. Bland's face.

"But if you really want this, Sara, you will have to prove to me that you want it bad. I hope you realize that we are talking about an exception that may seem unfair not only to those who have waited five years, but also to many others who have more experience than you do. You would be bypassing them all and getting ahead in the line."

"I understand. This is very kind of you. Anything, Mr. Bland. I'm a hard worker, you won't regret your decision."

"Define anything, Sara." Mr. Bland placed his right palm on Sara's thigh and stroked gently.

Sara froze. She sat frozen, staring at Mr. Bland's hand. He abruptly put his right index finger back on his lips and his thumb under his chin.

"Define *anything*, Sara," Mr. Bland said again.

Sara didn't say anything. Her head started to hurt.

After a long silence, Mr. Bland said, "Remember that you came to me, asking for help. You need to start speaking. I don't see much productivity in sitting here in silence. You and I both have work tomorrow morning."

Her head was really hurting now.

After another brief silence, Mr. Bland moved his hand to Sara's thigh again. This time, he slowly slid his hand up, pushing her skirt and exposing her white panties.

Sara closed her eyes. *This isn't happening. This isn't real. Let me just get up and leave.*

She opened her eyes. The room spun. Her head throbbed. She put her right hand on her forehead and tilted her head back. Mr. Bland moved closer to Sara and sniffed her neck, bit her earlobe, and jerked her head backward, pulling on the hank of her dark ponytail.

FIVE

Before that horrible nightmare, Gabriel had been very excited to be with Katie again. He had missed her terribly after she left the hospital.

They'd met at Mercy Hospital as fellow volunteers. She'd instantly become Gabriel's best friend. Katie was older; she would even qualify as a grown-up. He was big, too, but only in age. Gamma told him he would almost qualify as a grown-up if other people knew how old he was. But he liked not being a grown-up. It had perks.

He did not remember why he made Katie his best friend, but it didn't matter. She was his best friend and he looked forward to seeing her on Wednesdays and Thursdays. Those were the days when he worked at Mercy Hospital. It wasn't a complicated job. He helped patients like himself and others not like himself who did not have any companions.

He sat next to patients and either listened or talked to them.

Usually, he talked and patients listened. It was a good job, and above all a good break from staying home and hearing his Gamma and Pa yell at each other.

He would go back to school in the fall, but this was summer and he had nowhere else to go. The hospital job was a welcome break from the classroom. Sometimes he wished his mom and dad were alive. Maybe they would have sent him to a summer camp. Not that Gamma and Pa didn't love him. Gamma and Pa loved him . . . well, at least Gamma loved him; he didn't know what Pa thought about him. Gabriel imagined Pa must look at him the same way he looked at a wall. But both Gamma and Pa absolutely hated each other. They always fought. Gabriel just hoped for more peace in their house.

He didn't know who his father was, and his mother had died only a few days after he was born. Gamma did not like to talk about her too much and the one time Gabriel had asked about the cause of her death, there'd been a lot of shouting. He had stopped bringing up his mother's death with Gamma. But he brought it up with Katie.

Katie thought his mother may have died due to postpartum complications. He did not understand at first, but Katie explained there could be many complications in women's bodies during or after delivering a child. Gabriel wanted to know more. For the first time, he had someone patiently explaining to him what might have happened to his mother. Katie said she would Google and tell him more. She also told him that Google was a machine that could answer any question. Gabriel wished he could use Google, too. He had so many questions. But he could not use Google because he was blind.

Only partially though. While a blind person could not see anything, Gabriel could see a little. He could make out shapes—he could identify rectangles versus circles, tall versus short, fat versus skinny. He could also differentiate light from dark. Google wasn't something he could use, though; he couldn't read printed letters.

But Katie could, and she was very kind. She would use Google and answer Gabriel's many questions. Katie told him that the United States was the only developed country where the maternal mortality rate was on the rise. Maternal mortality was the grown-ups' way of referring to women dying after giving birth. She also told him that she found more than ten different complications, including heart problems and infections, that could lead to a woman's death after childbirth. She was sorry she couldn't tell Gabriel what exactly had caused his mother's death. It could've been any of the ten different complications she had found on Google, or something else altogether.

That was fine with Gabriel. At least now he knew his mother had died due to women's problem. When he grew up, he would help women with their problems so that other kids didn't have to live without their mothers. This thought made him sad. He had never known his mother, but he was sure she must have loved him so much. He loved her, too. He wondered how happy she must have felt after holding him in her arms. How she must have kissed him. He didn't remember anything from the day he was born, but he must have been so happy that day. Then, a few days later, his mother had died. He must have cried. She must have cried. How awful dying was!

SIX

One day, a nurse told Gabriel that Katie had left her job, and he wouldn't be able to see her at the hospital anymore. He was very sad. A few days after Katie stopped coming there, Gabriel told Gamma, who was also a nurse at Mercy Hospital, that he did not want to come to the hospital anymore.

He stayed with his Pa at home. Pa wasn't very good company though. Gabriel stayed in his room; Pa stayed in the living room. They ate separate lunches and did separate things until Gamma came home from the hospital. Then Gamma cooked dinner and they all ate together. Occasionally, without any quarreling. Although he didn't like his new life, he wasn't going back to the hospital. He missed Katie and the hospital reminded him of her too much. So, his room would have to do.

Soon he had a routine. He woke up in the morning, went to the kitchen and ate breakfast, came back to his room, went to the bathroom, went back to his room, went to the kitchen and ate the previous night's leftovers for lunch, came back to his room, went to the living room and greeted Gamma when she came home from work, went back to his room, came back to eat dinner with Gamma and Pa, and finally went to bed. That was pretty much it, day in, day out. Pa didn't say anything about how much time he spent alone, but Gamma was concerned. She said she was sad to see Gabriel "withdrawn." She didn't say this to Gabriel, but he heard Gamma say this to Pa one day. He wasn't eavesdropping, no no, Gabriel wouldn't do that. He knew he shouldn't listen to someone else's conversation.

One day while he was in his bedroom, he heard Gamma and Pa talking to each other like normal people, in a soft murmur. He was curious. When he stepped out of his room, Gamma and Pa's voices grew louder. They were talking quite politely to each other. Something very rare. That was all. He wasn't trying to listen to their conversation. Gabriel went back to his room after that and went on to thinking about Katie and their wonderful   conversations.

SEVEN

On July 31st, the day Sara disappeared, Chuck Lagano was waiting for her in the parking lot. She had told him she would clock out and "be right outside." Waiting in the car, Chuck was beyond excited; he was thrilled. He had offered Sara a ride home. She'd hesitated at first but then accepted his offer. How careless and gullible women can be, Chuck had thought. He was a customer she had just met for the first time. But neither Sara nor Chuck realized that this was their second meeting.

A few months before Sara disappeared, she had gone to Durable Furniture. She wasn't sure what had made her enter the furniture store. She wasn't looking for anything in particular. Her apartment wasn't big. It was 1050 square feet of space that she shared with her boyfriend. They had all the necessary furniture—a five piece dining set, one love seat, one three-seater futon, one TV, one TV stand, one bed, a couple of end tables, and one accent rug.

She reached a corner section with a limited collection of office furniture on display. She remembered that her boyfriend had wanted to set up a home office. Not that he needed a home office for his work, but just so that they had a little place where they could organize their important documents, something like that. Sara also liked the idea because she thought having a home office sounded elegant, even rich. In movies she had seen rich old men retiring to their studies after dinner. Anthony Hopkins in *Meet Joe Black* came to mind.

She looked around and saw a beautiful desk. The description read, "DURABLE FURNITURE EXECUTIVE DESK $599." *Not bad*, she thought. She had expected an executive desk to cost much more. But the rich old men she had seen in the movies probably did not shop at Durable Furniture.

"Can I help you with something?" she heard a voice say behind her.

She turned around and saw a middle-aged man in his late forties or early fifties. He had graying hair, wrinkled skin; he was thin and wore pants that were too big for him. The khaki pants were held up by a black belt. Perhaps the pants were from his heavier days. He was a store employee, she could tell by the logo printed on his blue polo shirt. Having worked in retail herself, she sympathized with the man. *The pay mustn't be much*, she thought. He couldn't even afford a new pair of pants after clearly losing a significant amount of weight.

"No, just browsing, thank you," she replied with a sweet smile.

"No problem. My name is Chuck Lagano. If you have any questions, please do not hesitate to call me, okay?"

Sara nodded. He turned and walked toward another customer who was standing by the mattress section. Sara did not ask any questions. She left the store with a sullen thought that she didn't have $599 to splurge on a stupid desk. Even if she did have money, their tiny apartment didn't have any space for an office. *Maybe later*, she thought. *But how?* Her boyfriend made more money than she did, but not enough. They didn't share their finances, so how much he made didn't really matter. He believed in keeping their finances separate, he had told her. She'd told him he was a selfish asshole. She didn't think he was the one but for the time being she was stuck with him. She thought about Arun. It brought a smile to her face. Arun had his own baggage, though. Her smile faded away.

It had been a brief meeting between Chuck and Sara. They both didn't think enough about it for their brains to register a memory. However, the day of their second meeting, July 31st, would be engraved forever in their brains.

EIGHT

Acab stopped at the curb, in front of the gold building. A woman opened the door and covered her head with her purse. She tried to move quickly to avoid the rain but that proved difficult because of her heels. She walked through the revolving door and into the lobby. She wasn't sure what she was supposed to do next. She looked around. People were coming in through the revolving door and heading to the elevators on either side of the reception desk. They seemed to know where they were going. She saw a security officer talking on the phone behind the reception desk, so she walked up to the desk.

The officer behind the desk was still on the phone and didn't seem to be in any hurry. "That was crazy . . . Luza didn't tell anyone she was coming and when she arrived . . . man, you should have seen Marcus' face . . . Hey man, I gotta go, I will see you in the evening . . . aight." He finally hung up the phone.

"Yes, ma'am! How can I help you?"

"I have an appointment with Mr. Michael Carter at 11 AM . . . well, in the next 15 minutes. I wasn't sure which floor; do I need a badge or something?"

"Where does Mr. Michael Carter work at?"

"I am not sure I understand. I was hoping you could tell me that."

"Which company? I need to know which company this Mr. Carter works for before I can tell you which floor he might be on. There are fifteen different companies in this building."

"Oh, of course! Carter & Spitz LLC," she replied.

"They are on the fifth floor. Once you get there, I suggest that you call Pam Knight from the intercom outside the door. Pam is one of their secretaries and can let you in and probably help locate this gentleman as well."

"Umm . . . ok . . . thanks!" She turned left and walked toward the elevators.

"That will be elevators on the right," announced the security officer.

On the fifth floor, a middle-aged woman wearing a white skirt and a tan blouse opened the door.

"Hi, Pam Knight. Nice to meet you. Please come in."

They shook hands and then passed a series of long hallways with rows of cubicles on either side.

"Mr. Carter is slightly running late. I will show you the conference room. Please make yourself comfortable there and he will join you shortly, okay?"

She nodded.

They turned right a couple of times and then a left. Pam finally stopped in front of a room with a small tag near the door that read, *Work Room 5.*

"Here it is. Would you like anything to drink?"

"No, I am all set for now. Thank you very much, Pam."

"You are very welcome."

They shook hands and Pam went back the same way she came. How people navigated this labyrinth of an office was a mystery to her.

She had been volunteering at a local hospital for a few months and it had been good for her. It felt good to help others. She was alive again.

Amazingly, she had been helped as well. Gabriel had an amazing aura. She felt at peace whenever she was with him. They would eat lunch together sometimes, sometimes they would just chat. He didn't know but he had helped her. She had enough energy now to look for jobs again.

She wasn't much of a news reader, but she saw plenty of newspapers at the hospital. One day when Gabriel wasn't at work—he only worked Wednesdays and Thursdays—she had grabbed one of the newspapers and sat in a corner of the cafeteria to eat her lunch. The same cafeteria where she had met Gabriel for the first time.

> "Hi! My name is Gabriel, I'm a boy. Who are you?" he asked.
> "Katie," she said merrily.
> "Hi Katie! Can I sit next to you and eat my lunch?"

She'd flipped the pages aimlessly for some time, reading a story here, a story there. Then under the classifieds section, she'd seen this ad. Carter & Spitz LLC were looking for a secretary for their client. The applicant needed to have a flexible schedule and the availability to travel all over the world. Compensation would be discussed during the interview. She had done plenty of different types of jobs before but had never done a secretarial job. She had been about to move on to other ads when her eyes fell on a portion of the previous ad: *travel all over the world.* Traveling the world and being away from Hartford sounded particularly appealing to her at the moment. She thought about it again. How difficult could a secretarial job be anyway? So, she typed the web address into her phone, finished her lunch, and went back to work. Later that evening, she applied online.

Today at the gold building, it was her third round of interviews. The first round had been over the phone. She had talked to someone on Michael Carter's team, who explained that they would need to complete a background check right away. This was a little odd, she'd thought. Normally, background checks were performed after the offer was made and it was accepted. But the gentleman who worked for Mr. Carter had explained that this criterion had been set by their client. It had to be done before moving to the next round of interviews.

When she'd asked who their client was, he said he couldn't disclose it at this time. It would be disclosed during the final interview. She'd asked why all this secrecy for a secretary position? He'd explained that their client was a high-profile client and needed a high level of discretion from their secretary. The secretary would have access to a lot of confidential information and they wanted to make sure their interests were always protected. If she was selected for a second interview, Michael Carter would explain more to her, he'd promised. He'd also said that it looked like she hadn't attached a photo on the online application. They would need a full-size business professional portrait for consideration. Again, she thought this was unusual for a secretary job, but she reminded herself of the opportunity to be away from Hartford.

She'd landed a second interview with Michael Carter at a downtown restaurant. Michael had ordered a salad, so she'd done the same. Michael was in his early fifties, balding in the front, and very tall. He'd asked her what she thought about the role so far. She'd told him she didn't know much about it yet, apart from the fact that it was a secretarial job with an expectation of flexible hours and availability for travel. The gentleman who had conducted her phone interview asked her to direct her questions to Michael if she was selected for the second interview round. Michael had looked up and smiled.

"I am sorry if we appeared too secretive to you," he said. "It is the nature of our client's business. But I can certainly tell you more than what you learned on your first interview . . .

"Our client is a high-profile executive who has businesses and interests all over the world. He needs a secretary who can keep up with his busy schedule. Your job would be of a typical secretary—manage his calendar, take notes, accompany him wherever he travels . . . you will have a busy schedule and won't get as many days off as you would get at other jobs. You will get Sundays off, if you are not traveling. Otherwise, you get two weeks paid time off annually.

"On the bright side though, our client travels to exotic places all the time and you will accompany him. If you like that kind of lifestyle then you won't be disappointed at the lack of PTO at all."

She smiled.

"How is it sounding so far? You think you can handle this kind of life?"

"I am certainly considering it," she said. "Travel sounds appealing . . . I haven't travelled much but have always wanted to . . ."

"Well . . . in that case, this job may turn out to be play rather than work for you . . ."

She smiled again, sipped some water, and worked on her salad with the tines of the fork.

"There is one more condition before we bring you in for the third and final round of interviews,"

She looked up.

"You will need to sign a non-disclosure agreement with us. This is again to protect our client and his interests."

She furrowed her brow and gave Michael a puzzled look. He reached for his bag and took out what looked like a book. He pushed it toward her.

"You will need to read this, understand it, sign it and bring it back to us."

Michael stayed quiet for a few seconds and said, "This does look intimidating, I agree. But I can summarize what is written in here. It basically says you will keep everything about this job confidential. Anything going forward would be just between you and us, starting with your third interview, when I will let you know who our client is. You cannot disclose who your employer is, where you are traveling to, anything you learn about our client, anything you do for our client . . . everything would be confidential."

Michael paused for a few seconds again and continued, "If you agree to this, then, well, the sky is the limit for you. We have already discussed the travel perks, but your salary would be out of this world. You will be paid $3000 a week for your services. That is $12,000 per month." Michael paused again and looked for her reaction.

She was stunned. She had never heard of that kind of money before. She couldn't believe she was being offered this salary for a secretarial job.

He smiled.

"I know this is a lot to take it in, but don't worry: you will have time to decide. Enjoy your lunch . . . you can take the NDA with you and bring it back later if you think you would like this kind of lifestyle. There are a few more caveats to your job, which I can only disclose after you sign and return this to us." Michael said, pointing to the non-disclosure agreement.

She raised the glass of water and finished it this time. Her hands trembled, ice rattled the glass as she put it back on the table.

She went home that night and read the agreement in detail. She didn't understand all the legal jargon, but she understood the overall theme. They would pay her ridiculous amount of money and in return she would have to give up her rights.

What's the catch? she wondered.

Today she'd come back for the third and final interview. She wasn't sure if she was happy or nervous. Her mind and her heart were not in the same place. Her heart wanted her to get up from the conference room table and leave. Her mind reminded her of a new life, away from Hartford.

Michael Carter finally entered the conference room, apologized for being late, shook her hand, and sat across from her. She pushed the signed NDA toward him. He smiled.

"Thank you for coming in today and I am glad you decided to sign the non-disclosure agreement."

She smiled.

Michael then continued, "I just want to remind you that we haven't offered you a job yet. At this point there are a few more things I would like to discuss with you, but since you already signed the agreement I can be more forthcoming with you . . .

"So, are you in a relationship?" Michael asked nonchalantly.

She was taken aback. She frowned and asked, "Why is that relevant to this job?"

"Well . . . if it wasn't relevant, I wouldn't have asked," Michael said.

She didn't say anything. She avoided eye contact with Michael. After a brief silence, Michael said, "Since our client travels a lot, we prefer his secretary to not be in a relationship. This is something we have learned from experience. With the amount of travel this job requires, it is bound to create friction with significant others. Hence, we require the secretary to be single." Michael paused and studied her.

"You don't look satisfied with my answer," Michael noted.

She hesitated and said, "Well . . . it is . . . it is . . . not . . . just not what I expected. That's all."

"What is?" Michael asked.

"Sorry?" she asked.

"What is it that you didn't expect?" Michael asked.

"Mm . . . why my relationship status would be important for a job. That kind of question . . . I think your explanation makes sense now . . . the amount of travel you describe does sound like a lot . . . I would have a problem with that too if my significant other were to travel that much."

"I agree," Michael said. "If you ask me, I wouldn't do it if I were offered this job. Simply because I have a wife and two daughters, and this kind of lifestyle wouldn't suit me and my family. This is mostly suitable early in one's career and in this case when you are single. But that is why I asked you during our lunch if this lifestyle would work for you . . . and you had indicated so. Is that still the case?" Michael asked, raising his eyebrows.

"Oh . . . yes, yes . . . this works." she answered.

Michael slowly nodded and said, "So what is it?"

"I don't understand?" she asked.

"Relationship?" Michael asked.

She was silent for a few seconds and then said, "That won't be a problem."

Michael raised his brow and looked at her. She lowered her eyes. He smiled.

"Ok. I will leave it at that," he said. "I would also suggest that if you are paying for your apartment and if it is expensive, you may want to switch to a smaller, cheaper unit." Michael leaned forward and continued, "You won't spend much time in Hartford, so why waste all that money on an apartment that you are not even going to use?"

She nodded.

"Ok . . . now about our client. Like I told you before, he is a very busy man who travels all around the world. He is extremely rich and is used to getting whatever he wants." Michael paused and looked at her.

She was listening attentively.

Michael continued, "He has certain habits that might . . . well . . . make people uncomfortable . . . especially women . . ." He paused again and studied her reaction.

She cocked her head, frowned, and continued to listen curiously.

"Well . . . let me cut to the chase . . . you have already signed the NDA, so what we discuss here cannot leave this room anyway . . . right?" He looked at her for her agreement.

She looked confused. He raised his eyebrows. She nodded reluctantly.

"He is a very touchy-feely individual . . . and tends to show his admiration and appreciation that way . . . so, you will get lots of hugs, pecks on your cheek, even a little tap on your behind . . . you know, like you see football players and coaches do." He paused again.

What the hell!

She didn't say anything.

"When you are traveling with him and he invites you to his room, he might just be in his bathrobe, or in his boxers, or in nothing at all . . . you will need to be comfortable with that . . . you can probably understand now why we had you sign NDA before discussing these habits of our client. If we hire someone and they do not find these behaviors acceptable, they could complain and that would not look good for our client. Now that you have signed this NDA, you can choose for yourself if you are open to these idiosyncrasies or not. If yes, great, you will make lot of money that you cannot make anywhere else. If your answer is no, we will move on to other candidates. Simple as that."

Her face turned red; her eyes widened. Michael met her eyes. She lowered her gaze.

That's the fucking catch! Why am I so stupid? I should have continued to volunteer at the hospital instead of coming here.

"One more thing . . . he may come on to you . . . you know. That will be up to you though. If you respectfully decline, he will back out. Or if you are feeling lonely and don't mind it, he will take that as well. But at any time, he will honor your wishes . . . like I said earlier, apart for his usual touchy-feely nature, he will always respect your desire."

Oh my god!

Michael studied her again.

She now maintained a stern demeanor. They both sat in silence. She picked her purse up from the floor, placed it on her lap, and asked, "Who is your client?"

"That would be the chairman of the Bland Corporation, Mr. Roman Bland."

NINE

After Chuck's first meeting with Sara, he had walked over to a woman who was standing in front of a Serta mattress. "Could I be of any help?" he asked. She gave him the same answer Sara had given only moments ago. Nothing unusual for Chuck. He told himself that he could only control doing his part—i.e. being polite and asking customers if they needed help. He couldn't force them to talk to him and ask him questions like the management wanted. Whenever he was a customer, he wanted peace and privacy and hated sales agents who appeared too keen on helping. *Leave me alone* was what he would think. He believed many customers who came into the store were also like him; they wanted to be left alone.

But of course, his theory couldn't be correct. If it were, star sales associates like Ashley Dupree wouldn't be successful. He did not know what magic she possessed. She would walk up to the same customer who had just waved him away and they would ask her all sorts of questions. It felt like playing a slot machine, not hitting anything for hours, then as soon as he left, Ashley took his seat and JACKPOT! Whatever her powers were, they clearly differentiated her from the pack. She'd been the outstanding sales performer for the last thirty-five months straight. There were rumors that her hourly pay and commission bonus were ridiculously higher than the rest of the sales associates'. Management feared that their golden egg laying goose would decide to lay her egg somewhere else. How ironic, Chuck thought, that this so called golden egg laying goose was infertile. He chuckled at the thought. No, she did have a child, a son, but he didn't believe for a second that it was possible for that fat fuck to naturally conceive. She must have done some test tube shit. Unlike him, who had three boys, all naturally born. Not even C-section crap. He was proud. And Ashley Dupree was infertile and fat, morbidly obese in fact. Chuck indulged in these thoughts and felt content.

However, even Chuck had to admit that those were probably her only two regrets, being fat and infertile. She was worshiped at work. She travelled a lot, he could tell based on how many vacation photos she posted on Facebook. Even the test tube shit looked happy in those pictures.

He looked at his own life. Except for his naturally born kids, he didn't have much to be proud of. His back pain didn't help either. He used to take Advil three times a day, but the pain was getting worse. He had seen a pain doctor and had slowly progressed to stronger and stronger opioids. The doctor gave him a few options to take his medication; he could take it as a pill, spray, or subdermal. Chuck chose the pill; the other options sounded creepy to him. The stronger opioids were great. His body melted, all problems went away, but still he didn't take them too often. His life sucked, but he wasn't stupid enough to get hooked on things like that. But he didn't tell his doctors that he only took opioids occasionally. They had prescribed the drugs easily enough and Chuck was able to get a handsome price for them on the street. The stronger the opioid, the better the price. Unlike Ashley, Chuck wasn't going to get any bonus from Durable Furniture, so he had to improvise.

Opioids also came in handy when he met Sara for the second time on July 31st.

TEN

August 2016

R ide-O-Share continued to find themselves in hot water. It had only been a few months since CEO Tripp Wozniaki resigned due to mounting pressure from investors and board members. In his statement, he had said he resigned "so that the company can go back to building rather than be distracted with another fight." Prior to Wozniaki's departure, Ride-O-Share had been exposed for having a workplace culture that included sexual harassment, deceiving investors and partners, and deceiving law enforcement agencies worldwide. And now, a missing report had been filed with the Worcester Police Department in Connecticut that indicated that a Ride-O-Share driver may have been behind Sara Sardana's disappearance. When the police report was leaked to the media, the Worcester PD did not comment on the report or the leak. The company did, however, issue a brief statement saying it hadn't been contacted by any law enforcement officials regarding a woman's disappearance. All they knew was what had been reported by the news outlets.

But that wasn't enough to stop the fury of bad news for Ride-O-Share. Their stock price was already at an all-time low due to months of negative publicity and the ousting of their founder and CEO. Soon after the news broke that Ride-O-Share had been linked to the disappearance of a twenty-one-year-old Connecticut woman, its stock nosedived into the biggest single day loss in history. Social media analysts who specialized in sentiment analysis reported a growing negative public perception about the company.

Faced with increasing public scrutiny and constant media coverage, Ride-O-Share issued another statement the next day stating that they had been contacted by law enforcement agencies regarding a woman's disappearance and that they were fully cooperating. They underscored that at this point neither the company or any of its drivers were under investigation. Police, on the other hand, were conspicuously mute on whether Ride-O-Share may have had a role in Sara's disappearance.

Although Worcester PD had been holding news conferences frequently, it wasn't until four days after Sara's disappearance that they finally broke their silence with regards to the ride sharing company. Ross Anderson had filed a missing persons report on August 1st at 2:15 PM stating that his girlfriend, Sara Sardana, had been missing since the day before. He had last spoken with her at 3:33 PM on July 31st for less than a minute. He claimed that she had asked him to pick her up from the Promenade shops at the Greenmile Walk where she worked. He had asked if she could take a Ride-O-Share instead and she had replied that she would do so. When she did not come home, he had tried to call her several times. Unable to find her, he tried to reach out to her family, who he hadn't spoken to in months. He was avoiding them because Sara had told him that they didn't approve of their daughter dating a white man, much less living with him prior to marriage. Sara hadn't been in touch with her parents lately either. After Ross called and the police contacted Sara's parents, they were in total shock. Sara was their only daughter. They cried. They pleaded publicly to Sara's presumed captors. Ross had tried to offer comfort, but Sara's parents were furious. They gave a thundering interview to a local reporter claiming Ross's involvement in Sara's disappearance.

Based on Ross's statement, Worcester PD had reached out to Ride-

O-Share and asked if they could confirm Ross's statement. The company had found Sara's profile in their database but there was more than just her profile; there was an entire history of every ride she had ever requested. Six hundred and five in total. But what wasn't in the database was any ride request made on July 31st, the day Sara disappeared. Police ended their statement saying they were still investigating and would report back as new information became available.

A reporter followed up by asking if the police had concluded that Ride-O-Share and/or any of its drivers had nothing to do with Sara's disappearance. The company's PR department had hoped that "Yes" would be their answer but the Chief of the Worcester PD announced "No," emphatically. He told the reporter that they hadn't concluded anything. All they were reporting were facts that could be disclosed to the public without compromising the investigation. They would continue to talk to everyone and anyone that could be associated with Sara, including Ride-O-Share and its drivers if needed.

This news conference certainly did not help to ease the company's miserable week. The internet buzzed with conspiracy theories. One theory speculated that Ride-O-Share had found out that one of its drivers had been responsible for Sara's abduction before police contacted them. To safeguard its reputation, the company had decided to delete the ride request log from its database. After all, the theory concluded, this wouldn't be the first time Ride-O-Share had been involved in illegal activity.

The theory cited a news article titled: **How Ride-O-Share Deceives Authorities Worldwide.** A popular news outlet reported a story from Seattle, Washington, where Ride-O-Share had started ride-share service without permission from city officials. The ridesharing was later declared illegal in Seattle and city officials wanted to build a case against Ride-O-Share by posing as riders, so they could catch the drivers in the "act." However, Ride-O-Share was one step ahead of them and had used a tool called Crystalball to tag ride requests that came from law enforcement or city officials. Once tagged, or "Crystalballed" in Ride-O-Share's lingo, the app would show fake information on the requestor's phone, indicating that a fake car was on the way but then the request would be cancelled. This allowed Ride-O-Share drivers to evade capture and made it difficult for law enforcement to catch them in the "act" and build a case against Ride-O-Share. The article did not conclude that Ride-O-Share had done anything illegal. **Ride-O-Share Deceives Authorities** was the title of the article itself, but the news outlet didn't go as far as to call Ride-O-Share's activities illegal. The conspiracy theorists, however, were not as considerate.

It was a serious accusation. The legality of Ride-O-Share's tools like Crystalball could be argued one way or the other. But there was no question about the legality of an abduction. What these conspiracy theorists had essentially implied was that there was a meeting in Silicon Valley where all the most powerful people sat around a table and decided that Sara's log from the day of her disappearance had to be deleted from the database to safeguard the company's reputation. When someone had replied to these theories, calling them "Outrageous, impossible in today's day and age," the conspiracy theorists simply replied with a picture and a caption, "King Trump, Duke of Manhattan, and Princess Ivanka, of the United Kingdom of America." A short message followed the picture: "Nothing is impossible."

There were other theories too. A crazy Ride-O-Share driver had abducted Sara simply because . . . he was crazy. The gender of the crazy was clear to the folks who proposed this idea—it had to be a man. Crazy men were capable of terrible things, the theory explained, and they didn't need any motive for their actions. These theorists sought support by citing a bitter story that also took place in the state of Connecticut. Only a few years before, twenty kids and six adults had been murdered at Sandy Hook Elementary School. No reason, no motive, just plain crazy.

Crazy was possible. What Arun found hard to imagine was an entire company involved in Sara's abduction or in the subsequent cover up. But then, the whole company wouldn't have to be involved, would it? A few "important people" or just one person who may have wanted to harm Sara, in theory, could've conspired without the knowledge of 99.9% of the company. If this was true, what kind of mess had Sara gotten herself into to earn the wrath of these "important people?" For all Arun knew, Sara couldn't have possibly gotten into such mess. She was a normal young girl, with a normal life. He was the only abnormal thing in it.

ELEVEN

November 2016

A run woke up, made himself coffee, and turned the TV on to the channel 7 news. Sara's disappearance was still being covered, but her story now occupied only the bottom portion of the screen with other flash tickers. Today it read, "South Hampton missing girl: authorities baffled, no lead." There was a time when you couldn't turn on the TV without seeing her story on every channel. But the media had moved on from Sara. She was probably dead by now, they had concluded.

Statistically speaking, they had a point. The odds of finding a missing person alive diminished drastically with each passing day. Today was day ninety-five. Her lifeless body might've been lying at the bottom of the Connecticut river, chained to a heavy object, a piece of metal, or a rock. Trout or bass probably made sure that her body didn't surface. Arun didn't want that to be Sara's fate, but he had to be pragmatic. Whoever had done this, for whatever reason, had gotten away with it. This wasn't ok. This was fucked up.

His heart beat faster and his head ached as her name disappeared on the TV screen. He hoped this wasn't anyone's deed after all. He hoped Sara had left on her own. Maybe she was sick of her life, sick of her good-for-nothing boyfriend. Maybe she wanted everyone to think she had disappeared. Maybe she wanted her boyfriend to be blamed, like everyone already had. If so, she was the one who had gotten away with this.

Arun sighed. No matter who was to blame, he couldn't let it go. He had to find out.

Since she'd disappeared, he couldn't get Sara out of his mind. He knew he had to move on. It seemed like everyone else had, including the police. Arun's last hope was *the stopped car*.

But Detective Jim Kelly had called again last night to inform him that this was a dead end, too. Jim wouldn't elaborate on what they had or hadn't found. Ongoing investigation, he had said. A common excuse police kept using that Arun had learned to live with.

Arun didn't trust Jim's investigative abilities, but since Sandra was with him, Arun was satisfied. That didn't mean he wasn't furious, though. Fuck "ongoing investigation." If it weren't for him and his theory, this investigation would be long dead and inches closer to becoming a fucking cold case.

Jim had asked Arun to feel free to contact him if something needed to be discussed, but by calling him first and not barging into the police department like Arun had done. Arun had grunted something that sounded like he understood and then hung up. He'd really wanted to say that the "barging in" business had provided them a lead, which Jim's incompetent force had been unable to produce. But he'd held his tongue.

No matter how much Arun disliked Jim, he knew he couldn't do anything on his own. He had to rely on the police if he wanted to find out what had happened to Sara. Slowly, it was becoming clear to Arun that the media could move on to another story, the police to another case, and even the world to a 5th dimension, but Arun couldn't move away from Sara. He had to know. He couldn't betray her. Again.

It was late morning now and Arun felt suffocated inside his apartment thinking about his latest conversation with Jim Kelly. He stepped out to clear his head. He walked around aimlessly for a while thinking about the stopped car. He thought about Sara, too. If not in the stopped car, where did she go?

It was a bright morning with clear skies. Sun shone directly on Arun's face. His head ached. Perhaps the sun was to blame. Perhaps all his jumbled up, non-stop thoughts. Perhaps he just needed to eat. He hadn't had breakfast yet. He looked around for a place to eat. He stopped. It was a twenty-minute walk from his apartment to the promenade shops at the Greenmile Walk. He couldn't believe he had walked for so long and was already standing on top of the hill overlooking the shopping center. It had been more than three months since he came here. Sara was last seen here.

But he was hungry, and the shopping center had a coffee shop that he liked. He was familiar with the shopping center. He had come here many times. Even with Sara. Come to think of it, how careless he had been with his rela . . . whatever it was with Sara. No, he wasn't the boyfriend that she might be trying to frame with her disappearance. Their . . . whatever it was . . . was, well, just complicated.

He saw the coffee shop to the left of the sidewalk and went inside. He ordered a macchiato and a bacon, gouda, and egg sandwich, to go. As he walked out of the coffee shop, he was looking down at the sidewalk, still thinking about Sara . . . then he saw the asphalt, then . . . BANG!

He felt hot liquid on his shoulder, smelled the strong smell of coffee, and heard a loud thud followed by a screeching sound. He felt no pain, but his head felt numb. It was getting dark outside. So dark, he couldn't see his own body. He squinted his eyes and opened them again. Nothing. He closed his eyes and patted his head several times. Nothing. Maybe it had gotten dark outside. He could hear though. He heard feet moving toward him, running. He heard a woman. She was saying something but then an alarm went off in monotone. The sound of the ringing alarm enveloped his body.

TWELVE

The next day

When Arun woke up in the hospital, there was nobody in the room. His headache was gone, and he could see. *Thank God.* His vision was still a blur, but only things far away seemed blurry. He moved his hand over his face and noticed he wasn't wearing his glasses. He must have dropped his glasses when . . .

When what? What had happened? He didn't remember. He remembered going to Greenmile Walk, he remembered getting coffee, and then the woman's voice . . . no, a woman yelling, she was yelling . . . what else? Oh, the blackness, a terrifying blackness. It wasn't like anything he had experienced before. Then suddenly, just like that, it came to him. He had banged his head on something and then blacked out, some woman was yelling at him, there were feet moving closer to him . . . wait . . . the feet had moved closer first and then the woman had started yelling . . . and then?

Arun thought for a minute. Nothing else came up.

The door opened, and a woman came in. "You are up!" she said, raising her eyebrows and backing up a little. "I should have knocked on the door before coming . . . sorry. I thought you were still . . . Sorry again." She came near Arun's bed.

"My name is Ann Horowitz. I am one of the nurses who is taking care of you since you had an accident." She paused, waiting for Arun's reaction.

Arun looked at her but did not say anything. Ann continued, "Do you know your name?"

"Yass." Arun cleared his throat and said again, "Yes. Arun Shah."

"Excellent. How much do you remember about what happened?"

"Not much. I remember walking out of the coffee shop with coffee and a sandwich and then my head . . . I think something hit me. I don't know what. There was darkness, I couldn't see. I panicked. I heard feet moving closer. A woman was yelling at me. That's about it. Next thing I know I'm in this room."

"Uh-huh. Okay, so let me tell you what the paramedics told us. You were hit by an SUV. Or rather, you hit the SUV. The witnesses told police that you walked down from the sidewalk into the road and kept walking, not looking at the SUV that was moving in front of you. Luckily it was a shopping center, so the SUV was moving slowly. You walked toward the moving SUV and hit your head on the side window behind the driver. You fell, hit your head on the road, and then became unconscious. Paramedics said you were still mumbling something unintelligible when they brought you here. Do you remember anything from the ambulance or after you were brought to the hospital?"

Arun shook his head.

"That's all right. After you were brought here, we put you through a CT scan. You had a concussion, but we didn't see anything else concerning. Your blood pressure was low, I now see that it is back to normal. Other vitals were fine. You were responding a little at that time. Do you remember any of that?"

Arun shook his head again.

The nurse smiled. "No worries. Amnesia is common after a head injury. We have you on pain meds but all in all, you look good to me, Mr. Shah. It could have been a lot worse."

She paused for a few seconds and said, "I'll send the doc in. He'll do some evaluations and we'll go from there. Okay? Any questions for me?"

Arun shook his head, again.

"Do you need anything? Water, anything to eat?"

"Water maybe," Arun replied.

"Sure. I'll bring water and I'll send the doc for your evaluation as well. Okay. See you in a bit."

Ann went out cheerfully and closed the door behind her.

Arun put his head back on the pillow. He didn't have much on his mind. Maybe it was the effect of the pain medication, even the hospital bed felt comfortable. All the thoughts he'd had before the accident were gone. He felt at peace; his head was lighter. Soon he dozed off again.

THIRTEEN

Chuck's second meeting with Sara wasn't really planned either. He had looked forward to July 31st, but only because it was his day off after ten straight work days. His three boys were at their grandparents' house and his wife was at work. He had the day to himself. The weather had cooperated, too. Besides the obvious, there was one additional perk of a day off: Chuck wouldn't have to see the fat pig, Ashley Dupree. Sometimes he wondered if she thought about him as much as he thought about her. She didn't. He didn't know.

Ashley didn't have time to waste on a nobody like Chuck. Ashley's life was her work. There're two types of people in this world: those who work to live, and those who live to work. Ashley was the second kind. The store didn't open until 9 AM on weekdays and 10 AM on weekends, yet Ashley was at work by 8 AM, six days a week. She took Sunday off and that was only because her management pleaded with her. Other sales associates grumbled because she always had a day off, every week, on a weekend. They sometimes didn't get a day off until they'd worked ten to fifteen days. But they couldn't say anything to their management. They knew what time she came and what time she left, always after the store closed. No sales associate could imagine being able to handle hours like that; most of them had families and they didn't care much about *Durable Furniture* anyway.

Ashley had family too. She lived nearby with her husband and son. It wasn't that she didn't care about her family, but rather that she liked her job too much. For some, sales associate might not sound like a very likeable job, but for Ashley it was her temple. She loved everything about it. Most of all she liked being able to sell to reluctant customers. She could even sell to customers who were not looking to buy anything. It was a gift, she knew. She also knew that other sales associates were more than just envious. She loved it. She could easily be the greatest saleswoman that had ever lived. This thought made her sad. Unfortunately, in today's world you were not considered the greatest anything unless you were up high in the corporate chain of command. Steve Jobs was considered the genius sales guy, but she knew without a doubt that if Steve and she were in a duel, Steve wouldn't stand a chance.

But of course, she couldn't rouse the dead just to make her point, and neither was she a corporate type. Sitting all day long in a fancy chair and looking busy in the name of creating sales strategy wouldn't be something she would enjoy. She liked hands-on, roll up your sleeves and get down to business type of work. Her on-the-floor sales job was what she wanted and there was no one in the whole wide world who could beat her at that. The world would never know her genius because she didn't plan to go corporate, but it was enough for her that she knew, her managers knew, and above all, her envious colleagues knew.

Besides, her management had treated her way too well for her to be thinking about anything else. The pay was probably the best an on-the-floor sales associate could ask for. She would've even done it for much less, but of course she did not disclose that. Let them think that she would leave if others paid more. She would've gladly spent even more time at the store but that was where her management had drawn the line. She had hoped to convince them, but they were much too familiar with her sales tactics. There was a reason behind her insistence, though. She didn't want to stay at home.

She loved her son and loved spending time with him, but that also meant seeing her husband and his pathetic existence. She wasn't sure who hated whom the most. She hated the fact that she was clearly the most hardworking, but ironically, he made the most money. Fucking corporate jobs. He probably hated her weight, she thought. Hate was perhaps too strong a word to describe how they felt about each other; lack of love was probably more accurate. No matter how you described it though, the fact was that they hadn't had sex in the last six months. Their no-sex, no-love relationship meant their marriage was probably over. But they didn't admit that yet. Not that the thought hadn't crossed their mind, of course it had. But they told themselves that it wouldn't be fair to their son. He deserved to grow up with both parents. So it was. They stayed under the same roof, ate at the same table, slept in the same bed, but as strangers. Work reminded Ashley of her accomplishments; home reminded her of her failures.

FOURTEEN

November 2016

Arun had plenty of time in the hospital and nothing to do. Sara visited in his thoughts often but unlike very recently, these thoughts were pleasant. He thought about the first time he met her.

It was in a mall, three years ago. Worcester Hill Mall was a regular mall one would find in most cities and towns. It wasn't like the Promenade shops at the Greenmile Walk, where Sara had last been seen on July 31st. Promenade shops at the Greenmile Walk was upscale, overflowing with boutique shops. All of the shops were only one story high and the landscape was meticulously maintained. The buildings that housed these shops had columns and arches that resembled the architectural styles of the Romans and the Greeks. Worcester Hill Mall, on the other hand, was one large boxy building with two floors that housed Macy's on one end and Sears on the other, with small shops distributed throughout the middle section of the building. Not much to look at from an aesthetic point of view.

It was Sunday afternoon. Arun was at his usual hair salon for a bi-weekly ritual. As he walked in, he saw four chairs in the waiting area of the salon. Two were occupied. He walked up to the register. A hair stylist was sweeping hair off the floor, facing away from Arun. Eventually, she looked behind her, out of habit perhaps, and noticed him. He gave her a smile. She came toward the register and asked how she could help. He said he needed a haircut. She asked if he had been to the salon before. He nodded. "Phone number?" she asked. Arun gave her his phone number. She looked him up on her computer. She hesitated for a minute.

Arun understood her dilemma and said, "Arun Shah."

She nodded and tapped the screen in front of her with her index finger. She looked at him and said it would be about a ten minute wait. He thanked her and turned around. Still four chairs in the waiting area and two were occupied, but this time Arun also noticed that one of the empty chairs wasn't actually empty. A Starbucks coffee mug sat on the chair. Arun assumed it belonged to the girl who sat in the adjacent chair. To her left was now the only empty chair. A man was sitting to the left of the empty chair.

Arun hesitated for a minute, unable to decide if he should sit or not. All four chairs were tightly placed, and if he decided to sit, the three of them would be sitting shoulder to shoulder. He looked at the other end of the floor to see if there were more chairs. During his past visits, he had noticed a few more chairs in the opposite corner. None today. He looked at the empty chair again. *What's wrong with just standing?* he thought. After all, the stylist said it was going to be only ten minutes. He spent some time in this state of indecision, then walked over and sat. As he had expected, it was snug but not as bad as he had thought. None of them were too large to cause space issues.

A minute later the man sitting next to Arun was called. He walked over to the stylist's chair and told her he wanted a number 4 or 5 at the back and scissors on top. The stylist asked if it was 4 or 5; he replied that he wasn't sure. Arun couldn't see the stylist's face, as she was standing directly in front of Arun, facing away from him. He wondered if she was rolling her eyes, thinking, *Well, I can't give you a 4 or a 5, can I?* After a brief silence, she said, "4 is shorter than 5, you know?" Arun didn't know if she was patronizing or just trying to help the guy, but it worked. The guy quickly replied that he wanted a 4. No matter what the stylist's intention might have been, she clearly knew what needed to be said so that her customer could come to a decision.

"How long did she say?" Arun heard a voice from his right.

He turned and saw a beautiful young woman with dark hair and lovely eyes. *Are those natural eyelashes or fake ones?* he wondered. Her eyelashes were of such size that they could have been natural, but one wouldn't be able to tell the difference if they were not.

Her face looked soft and unblemished. Her skin tone wasn't white, or yellow or brown. It was somewhere between lighter caramel and darker vanilla, which blended perfectly with her dark hair and bright brown eyes.

While Arun made eye contact with her, his peripheral vision decided to take a . . . little tour. He noticed a body-fitting pink hoodie. Her breasts were small and suited her age. But what was her age? She looked young, but that didn't mean anything. He had met many women who were older and looked young. On the other hand, she could actually be young. She could actually be in high school. That thought suddenly shut off his peripheral vision and he gave full concentration to her attentive eyes.

"I am sorry, how . . . umm . . . what?" he replied. Somehow her voice had entered his ear and yet his brain did not translate that sound wave into something coherent. He wasn't sure whether to attribute it to his inattentiveness or the impact of her stunning beauty.

"I was asking, how long did she say?" she repeated.

Thankfully, this time Arun's brain translated the sound waves correctly and quickly. "She said ten minutes," he replied.

"Oh, that's not bad. I entered my name, went around the mall for forty minutes and have already waited ten more minutes in this chair," she said.

"Wow! That reminds me," he said, "last time when I was here, I brought a book with me so that I could do some reading. Like it was for you today, I thought I would have to wait a long time and wanted to utilize my . . . time. That day, I waited only five minutes." He smiled and added, "Today, I don't have a book."

"It's only ten minutes so you should be okay," she said.

Arun only nodded.

After a brief awkward silence, she said, "Despite the wait, I like it here. Good place. Good people."

Arun nodded again and muttered an agreement under his breath.

"I don't come here often though. It is expensive, you know. Twenty dollars for a haircut?" She continued to speak, now with widened eyes, "But my hair doesn't grow quickly, so I don't really have to come often. Every four to six months maybe."

"That's not bad. I have to come here every two weeks, or my hair gets to a length I do not like," Arun replied.

"I guess men's hair is that way." She smiled in agreement.

Another awkward silence, but this wasn't as brief as the last one. Arun was staring at hair products next to the cash register, hoping one of the products would inspire a conversation topic. No luck. He felt that she was in a similar situation, searching for a topic. Of course, Arun did not have any means to verify that hypothesis. What she said next, however, emboldened it.

"This summer I paid the most I ever have for my hair, two hundred dollars," she said. Arun's eyes widened and he asked what that was for. "Perm. To get my hair like this." She pointed to her very beautiful wavy black hair. "It's naturally straight," she added.

Arun thought about telling her that it suited her well because it did. But no, he didn't say anything like that. "Oh ok," was all that came out of his mouth. He managed to add, "How long will it last?"

"Until all this grows out," she replied.

He did not understand. Arun had grown up in a family where his mother was the only female in the house. He had never heard of a perm or anything close to it in his life. He must have given her a puzzled look because she added, "When my hair grows back, it will grow back straight. My new hair will be straight and my old hair wavy. Eventually, straight hair will replace this wavy hair completely." That seemed to sadden her.

Arun understood now and asked, "And how long does that take normally?"

"Depends how fast your hair grows. The stylist said six months but mine grows very slow, so I think it will last eight to nine months," she said.

"Good," he replied.

It was time for another awkward silence. Arun was searching for topics again and found none, again. Finally, after almost a minute he asked, "What do you do?"

She looked puzzled and asked, "What do I do?"

"Yes," he said.

"Well, I work at Connecticut Grocery as a cashier while I put myself through college," she replied.

Thank God she said college.

"South Hampton Connecticut Grocery?" he asked.

She smiled and said curiously, "We are in Worcester Mall. Why did you think South Hampton?"

"I only named the one I go to when I have Connecticut Grocery needs."

She smiled and said, "Well, we may meet again then."

He smiled back.

"What are you studying in college?" he asked.

"Early elementary education at UConn-Hartford," she replied.

"Ah, kids then?" he asked.

"Yes, kids." She nodded with a smile.

"I work in Hartford too," Arun added.

"Oh yeah, where at?" she asked.

He named a large insurance company based in Hartford, Connecticut. On paper, this insurance company was headquartered somewhere else, where taxes were not as ridiculously high as they were in Connecticut. There had once been a time when Hartford was known as the insurance capital of the world. If one looked at any major insurance carriers today, you would still find Hartford DNA. But over the years, companies had slowly moved out. Other states were looking more business-friendly, a.k.a. tax-friendly, than Connecticut. But this insurance company still had its major operations in Hartford.

"I've heard that name before, but what do they do again?" she asked.

"Insurance," Arun replied.

"You work for an insurance company?"

There was real interest in her voice now. Whenever he announced the name of the company he worked for, he expected anyone in the state to recognize it, more so if you went to school in the city of Hartford. But he'd never expected elementary education majors to care much about the world of insurance.

"How did you get into insurance? Business school?" she asked.

"Well, that would be a normal way to get into the insurance world,

I guess. I took a detour. I completed my undergraduate degree in math and then finished graduate school in statistics. While I was in grad school, I also sat in for a few Actuarial exams. Basically, they test whether you understand the mathematical and statistical principles needed to run an insurance business. When it was time to look for jobs, it was insurance companies that were mostly interested in me. I liked this company among a few I interviewed with and five years later, I am still there," he replied.

"You like it?" she asked.

Arun hesitated for a second and said, "Well, it pays my bills."

She looked at him, confused. She said, "I like my job," as if Arun had said the exact opposite.

Arun surely didn't hate his job, but he didn't quite know how he truly felt about it either. He was very appreciative of what it had given him. What it had given to an immigrant who was only nineteen when he first came to this country.

FIFTEEN

He'd graduated from college in four years with a degree in Mathematics, but that did not mean much in 2009, at the peak of the great recession. People were getting laid off left and right. Even American citizens were having a hard time finding jobs, and he was an immigrant. An educated immigrant, but an immigrant nevertheless. Besides, for him to be able to find a job, an employer had to be willing to go through piles and piles of paperwork to successfully prove that Arun had exceptional skill sets, which were in high demand in the United States and couldn't be fulfilled by American citizens alone. Arun's job needed to be a dirty job that most Americans would refuse to do. Since Arun had graduated with a degree in mathematics, the jobs he was qualified for weren't literally dirty. However, they did meet the other criteria: a job that many Americans would rather not do. It involved numbers and calculations.

Graduating with a degree in mathematics might sound exceptional to many, but it didn't feel exceptional to Arun. He admitted he was good with numbers, very good in fact. He was awarded an outstanding student award by the Department of Mathematics and Computer Science when he graduated. But there was a difference between being good at something and being passionate. He envied those who knew what they wanted to do at a young age. "I've wanted to be a singer since I was four-year-old . . . I've wanted to fly on a rocket ship since I was ten . . ." YouTube was loaded with videos of people like these, who knew what they were passionate about. Arun only knew what he was good at. Passion was something he heard other people talk about.

After college, he got accepted into a graduate program in statistics. Still not out of passion but in line with what he was good at. Besides, there were three other reasons he chose statistics.

First, he had realized that his interests varied widely, from mathematics to genomics to economics. An advanced education in any one field would imply abandoning the others. The world had amassed so much knowledge that one could spend a lifetime studying just a tiny field. This troubled Arun. So, he searched for something that would unify his diverse interests. Eventually he landed on statistics. Not because statistics unified everything but simply because statistics was widely applicable in many disciplines. And in theory, at least, Arun didn't have to abandon anything.

Second, Statistics was a STEM discipline—Science, Technology, Engineering, and Mathematics. For an immigrant, there was an attractive reason to graduate with a degree in STEM. The United States Department of Labor agreed that not many Americans wanted to pursue a degree in STEM, a.k.a. America's other "dirty" job. Hence, there were many STEM jobs available to an immigrant.

Third, he graduated from college in 2009, and good luck finding a job during the great recession.

So it was. Arun pursued graduate studies in Statistics. A couple of years later, he graduated, the economy improved, and he landed a job as well. His employer successfully convinced the government that Arun's job was indeed America's "dirty" job. Arun didn't mind. This dirty job paid handsomely.

The job changed a lot of things in his life. Where he lived, what he drove, what he ate, where he ate, but it still couldn't change one thing: passion. He continued to excel at work, like he had done during his college and grad school days. He was consistently ranked an exceptional performer. He was good at his work, very good in fact. But still, he only knew what he was good at. Passion eluded him. It was something he heard other people talk about.

Arun couldn't explain all of this when the girl in the salon shop nonchalantly announced that she liked her job. He simply responded again with, "It pays my bills." He thought if they ever met again, he would explain it over coffee.

She nodded. "It pays your bills," she said.

This time, somehow, she seemed to be satisfied with his answer. He didn't think he'd said it any differently, but he saw a look on her face that seem to convey, "I understand." Maybe she was thinking "whatever." Either way, that was the end of that conversation.

SIXTEEN

Arun was about to say something else to the girl but was interrupted by another voice. It was a stylist, not the one who had pulled his name from the system, but a different one. She was calling his name. "Looks like I am next," Arun said sheepishly, got up, and followed the stylist to her station. As he approached her station, he realized that he had not said goodbye to the lovely young woman. A simple, "It was nice to talk to you," would have been adequate. Perhaps he could have introduced himself and asked for her name. There were many ways to end a pleasant conversation, the least polite of which was to just walk away when your name was called.

Arun's heart raced. He wasn't sure if it was due to regrets of how he'd left the conversation or due to something else. But he felt a sensation that he hadn't felt in a long time.

"What are we doing today?" the stylist asked.

"Three at the back and side and scissors on top. I like to part, so if you could leave most on the right side and shorten the left that would be great," he replied.

"If you want to part then maybe we shouldn't take anything off on the right side at all. You will probably be able to make it stay better if there is more volume," she said.

"Okay. Let's do that if you think that will help," he agreed. No point in telling a stylist how to do her job, he thought.

The clippers started to make their usual hum. Soon, his head felt lighter. Meanwhile, his mind was heavy. A thousand different thoughts were interacting at the same time. Nothing was coherent, except for the sensation in his heart. He noticed that the girl was called upon to take a seat at the station right in front of his, which meant he wouldn't be able to see her once she sat in the chair. However, before she sat down, as she stood up and came toward the station, he noticed a few more things he hadn't noticed before. She was wearing pink sneakers that matched her pink hoodie, and blue washed jeans covered her slender legs.

When his hair was done, he thanked his stylist, got up from the chair, and walked up to the cash register. As he passed by, he looked up at the mirror in front of him. Their eyes met; she smiled. He gave her a sheepish, half-committed smile back and jerked his head away, as if he had seen a forbidden object. At the cash register, he stood with his hands in his front pockets, then immediately took them out and folded his arms. After a few seconds, he put his hands back in his front pockets. His stylist hadn't joined him at the register yet. She was still over at her station sweeping his hair off the floor and putting it in a bin. He looked at the girl. Her station was now in front of him and only slightly to the left. She was busy talking to her stylist. He decided it was useless just standing and waiting for the stylist, so he went back to the waiting chair and sat.

"Are you paying now or are you paying together?" his stylist asked as she came toward the cash register. Arun looked to his left and noticed a new guy in the waiting chair next to him and thought, why would they pay together? Then he looked up at his stylist and noticed that she was pointing at the girl.

"OH NO. Not together," came out of his mouth. He immediately regretted it. OH NO, in particular, came out too strong and louder than he would have liked. When he said it, his eyes were wide open, his eyebrows were raised, his head was shaking, and his lips made a dramatic O. He answered as if someone had accused him of lying and he needed to quickly vindicate himself.

"Okay. Thought you and the young lady over there were together." The stylist shrugged.

He didn't say anything, just smiled nervously. He wished they were together too. Would that be appropriate? She looked young. Young enough to be underage. Prior to this day, Arun had never encountered a situation like this before and did not know what societal etiquette dictated regarding talking to underage girls. Was the expectation that he should ignore her because she was underage? Be rude in doing so? Was a polite conversation also frowned upon? He clearly did not know. For that matter, he didn't know if she was underage either. She had told him she was a freshman in college. A typical freshman could be anywhere between seventeen and nineteen. He was nineteen when he was a freshman, but there'd been a few in his class year who were not yet eighteen, creatively named "babies" by their older classmates. This girl could be a baby too. That frightened Arun. How incredible, he thought, that a mere thought of finding an almost eighteen-year-old female attractive felt like a crime in his head, yet a few months later it would be ok? If women matured faster than men, then wouldn't a seventeen-year-old young woman be equivalent to an eighteen-year-old young man? He abruptly stopped this train of thought because this wasn't going to help him one bit with his present dilemma.

Earlier, when he had said OH NO, his eyes had automatically peeked at the girl, perhaps looking for her reaction. She was still busy talking to her stylist. But he thought he had noticed a smile on her face when he uttered those regrettable words. It could very well have been his paranoia, but he thought she might have said, "Poor thing!"

"It will be twenty dollars for today," the stylist announced.

Arun added five dollars tip when prompted by the credit card processing machine, signed, thanked the stylist again, and hurried out. He felt relieved to be out of the salon. But his heart was still pounding. A million things were going through his head. Did he have a chance? Why didn't he ask her name? Would he see her again? Should he go to Connecticut Grocery tomorrow? Most importantly, was she underage? All these thoughts poured into his brain at the same time, so he couldn't concentrate on one at a time. His heart pounded even more at the idea of going to Connecticut Grocery and meeting her after work. He could head out of work early instead of following his usual routine back home. He could act casual, as if he was there to buy something. He could look for her and if he were to find her, he could act like it was a happy coincidence. After all, wandering away from home in the opposite direction to satisfy his heart's calling wasn't something he would be doing for the first time.

When Arun was fourteen, he rode on a school bus that headed in the opposite direction of his home, only because a girl he had liked since fifth grade rode on that bus too. It was a pain coming back home after this adventure, but it had been worth it. He'd lucked out and sat next to this girl. A few other kids from their class had joined and they all played charades until one by one, everyone got off the bus except for Arun. The driver turned around, looked at Arun, and said, "That was the last stop." Arun pretended to have missed his stop to his aunt's house and asked if the bus was going back to school again. When the driver said yes, Arun told him he would go back to school and call his aunt instead. He got off at the school and took a public bus back to his house. By the time he reached home, it was past dinner time. He had to lie and pretend one more time. But it had all been worth it.

Ironically, Arun had never mustered enough courage to ask that girl out in school. They'd both graduated from high school and gone their separate ways. That evening on the school bus was something Arun remembered fondly for a long time. It also made him wonder what would have happened if he had mustered enough courage. Would he have been happier? Would his life have been much better? He didn't know. Regardless of what might have happened and what that would have done to his life, he certainly wished there were more fond memories than that one evening on the school bus.

For this reason alone, he decided to go to Connecticut Grocery after work.

SEVENTEEN

September 2016

Katie was back. This time not as a real person, but as an apparition in Gabriel's dreams. He didn't mind at all. When they had both worked at Mercy Hospital, he would meet Katie for a few minutes a day or sometimes for an hour during lunch. That was it. Now, she visited his dreams every day. He was very happy.

But something was different. She was no longer the happy, friendly soul she used to be. She stared at the floor and only answered when he asked her something, but never started a conversation herself, like she used to. Dream Katie was sad and boring. But it was okay with Gabriel. Sad Katie was better than no Katie. Besides, it was only a dream. In real life, Gabriel hoped that Katie was much, much happier wherever she was. For now, he was just happy to have Katie back in his life.

Having Katie in his life and getting to talk to her in his dreams made him less . . . what was the word . . . *withdrawn* . . . yes, that was what

Gamma would say. He even asked Gamma if he could go back to Mercy Hospital again. Gamma said she had asked people at the hospital, but they had already filled his position. Gabriel was surprised. He asked Gamma: where did they find someone with special abilities like his? Gamma did not answer. Luckily, Gamma's old friend worked at a nearby hospital, Worcester Memorial, and she got him a volunteer job there instead. He would work only on Wednesdays and Thursdays, just like he had at Mercy Hospital, and since school had already started, he would only work after school. Gabriel was very excited that his new job was going to be similar. Sometimes he would meet old people with no children. Sometimes he would meet old people with children who were far away and could not come see their parents. Sometimes he would meet people with a terminal disease. That was the grown-ups' name for people who were going to die soon. It was different patients every time, but Gabriel was always ready. With great power came great responsibility, Gabriel always reminded himself.

Only one of his patients was a regular at this new hospital. His name was Simon Lucas. Simon was in a coma. Gabriel did not know why Simon was in a coma but that was not important to Gabriel. That was Doctor's job to figure out. Gabriel's job was to make sure Simon had someone to talk to. It was a different experience for Gabriel, that Simon wasn't doing much of the talking. Gabriel had to do the talking for the both of them; he was more than happy to. Every now and then Simon would open his eyes. The first time it happened, a nurse was also in the room. She told Gabriel that Simon had opened his eyes and went out to call a doctor. Gabriel looked at Simon's face carefully and noticed that as soon as the nurse left, something changed in his face. He later learned that Simon had closed his eyes and that was what Gabriel had noticed. Since then, Gabriel had become an expert at identifying closed and open eyes.

Simon opened his eyes many times after that. Gabriel wasn't sure if the subjects of their conversations made his eyes open or if it was something else. It was always unpredictable, so Gabriel did not think much about it. But one time when Simon opened his eyes, Gabriel was talking about Katie.

During his last visit, Gabriel had told Simon everything about Katie. He described her voice, her laughter, even how she looked. Gabriel did not know what Katie actually looked like. Nevertheless, he could describe what her shape looked like. Gabriel discovered that just like DNA, everyone's shape had a specific identity. He couldn't exactly describe how that worked but nobody had ever been able to deny his ability to identify people. All they had to do was line people up. Of course, the lineup had to be of people Gabriel already knew. No one could identify people they didn't know, duh.

Once people were lined up, Gabriel would identify every single one of them. For everyone else it seemed like magic, but for Gabriel, it was as natural as vision itself. There was just one tiny secret that Gabriel didn't tell everyone. Yes, he could identify people based on their shapes. But it wasn't 100% error free. When he was in doubt, he used his sense of smell, and that had never failed him. In his experience, there was only one human being that had both a particular shape and a particular smell.

Katie had the most amazing smell. Not her natural smell. Her natural smell was like anybody's. But her natural smell was always masked by the world's most amazing perfumes. Most of the time, perfume made it difficult for him to recognize people, since it masked their true natural smell. Gabriel had to get really close to make out the true scent beneath the overpowering smell of a perfume. If it was someone he already knew, it wasn't much of a problem. He would simply ask for a hug and once they were in his tight grip, forget about remaining anonymous. But with strangers or new acquaintances, he couldn't get close without making them uncomfortable. When that happened, he failed to create a profile of a distinct individual in his head, all because of a perfume. Ironically, even perfumes were not an issue when it came to recognizing Katie. She was the only distinct shape in the entire hospital who smelled so amazing. One didn't need Gabriel's special powers to recognize Katie.

As usual, Simon did not say anything while Gabriel described Katie at length. He explained his friendship, her kindness, and even her smell. Then he described how she had left Mercy Hospital for a paying job. Gabriel told Simon that he didn't blame Katie for leaving a volunteer job for a paid one. After all, everyone did not have a Gamma who earned and took care of them. As Gabriel started to describe his dreams, Simon opened his eyes again. It wasn't the first time, and Gabriel would soon learn it would not be the last. He wished it meant something, but even with his special powers, Gabriel could not decipher Simon's language.

He also told Simon that Katie seemed different now. The old Katie—who would always stop by and say hello as soon as she saw Gabriel, who kissed him on his cheek, who gave him advice and suggestions, who Googled Gabriel's questions—was gone. Now she had been replaced by the new version of Katie, who looked away from him down at the floor, who never came near him to say hello, and who only answered what he asked. Her style had also changed. When she had worked at Mercy Hospital, she wore clothes with all kinds of colors. Red, green, yellow, blue, always something colorful. Of course, he only saw the blurred colors, but it didn't take a superhuman to differentiate a blue blur from a red blur, duh. But now, she wore the same dress every night. Some mixture of orange, yellow, and brown with little black hems at the edges of the dress. But again, it was Gabriel's dream. Katie's fashion sense in his dream probably indicated his own fashion sense rather than hers. That thought made him chuckle.

EIGHTEEN

Chuck thought of himself as a chameleon. He wasn't apologetic about it; he was even proud. He thought the world had gotten chameleons completely wrong. Being a chameleon wasn't about lying or deceiving. It was all about adapting. Why would you blame the chameleon for changing its color to be safe from preying snakes? Shouldn't snakes share the blame? Chuck had lived among many snakes and it was pure experience that had taught him to adapt, like a chameleon. Adapt enough to survive. Survive among fat slithering bitches like Ashley.

Chuck was sure that one of the managers, either the store or regional, must've had a fat pig fetish to offer such special treatment to that bitch. Chuck proudly changed colors. The fat bitch probably thought he admired her because he showered praises when he was around her. But the only thing he admired about her was her huge jugs and the fact that underneath all the fat and layers, there was also a pink pussy. No matter how much he loathed her, he couldn't deny that if the opportunity presented itself, he would fuck her. Maybe he would come early so that she wouldn't get the satisfaction. That would make him happy, to fuck her and leave her hanging.

But it wasn't just fat Ashley. Chuck would fuck any . . . well . . . most women. There were clearly some whom he wouldn't even touch. A homeless woman, for example. He had once seen a homeless woman in NYC and had wondered if he would fuck her. She was young, and her face was decent enough. After a quick clean up, he imagined she would even look attractive. But he drew the line there. Who knew how many venereal diseases she might be carrying. He pitied her, a rarity for Chuck. What did nights in NYC look like for a young homeless woman? He wondered.

Then there were other obvious exceptions, such as old women in nursing homes. There were a few more exceptions like that, but that was what they were—a few exceptions. For the most part he was game as long as they came with a pair of boobs and a cunt. Ironic, he thought, that even with such a liberal philosophy and more than forty years of existence, he could count his sexual partners on one hand. Moreover, there'd only been one since he'd gotten married. He could have certainly paid for sex but for some reason hadn't been able to. Perhaps the same general issue with cleanliness or perhaps a fear of the unknown, getting caught by the police, beaten up by a pimp, etcetera, etcetera. Whatever it was, he had thought about paying for sex but had never done it. What he hoped for was to find ordinary women to fuck. Even fat pigs like Ashley would do, but normal and ordinary and certainly without commitment. Just fuck and go home. No drama, no more kids. God hadn't created him with the instruments to raise a child; he was only bestowed with an instrument he could use to fuck. That was God's wish, not his. It was a woman's job to raise a child, a rule he strongly enforced at home.

But unfortunately, ordinary women were probably getting sex somewhere else. Even fat pigs like Ashley were probably getting some action. Ashley for sure, after all she was married. He wondered what her husband looked like. Poor fellow had certainly drawn the wrong card, married a fat pig and then had to take care of her test-tube shit. This he assumed based on how much time Ashley spent at work. There was no way she was caring for that test-tube shit.

He couldn't live with the fact that fat Ashley's sex life might be better than his. This had to change. If not willingly, he was ready to use force. When Sara accepted his offer for a ride-share on July 31st, he thought this was his opportunity. He had waited long enough.

NINETEEN

One week before Arun met Sara at the salon three years ago, he had called in sick, again. Lately, he had been making one excuse after the other, whatever it took to get out of going to work. At first, he had wondered if this was some sort of clinical condition, like depression. But lately he had come to realize that he was just getting bored. He needed something different at work, perhaps even in life.

Going to work and browsing the web all day did not feel like the best use of his time. Not that he didn't have any work to do. The list of what he needed to do was expanding and even though he had employees to delegate work to, there was only so much he could delegate. After all, his intention wasn't to overburden anyone. The work that didn't get delegated had to get done as well. But he couldn't muster any energy. Soon, enough work had piled up that Arun dreaded going to the office and started making more excuses.

Today he was sick, a couple of weeks ago he'd had to pick someone up from the airport, and so on. He wasn't 100% lying most of the time. He indeed had to pick someone up from the airport, but on a Saturday, not on a Monday like he had said. Since it wasn't 100% made up, he told himself it was okay. But there was no getting around calling in sick. He wasn't sick; in fact, he felt great. That was more proof to him that it wasn't anything clinical. He just needed a change.

When he did go to work, it became even more apparent to him that he didn't like what he was doing. He spent his days browsing the web or taking walks around the city. Arun's favorite place to walk was at the park, in front of the Connecticut State House. It was a beautiful area with plenty of greenery. The back lawn of the State House offered a lovely view of downtown Hartford. There were not many people Arun knew of who thought highly of Hartford, especially the downtown area. But at least from the State House looking toward the UnitedHealth building and then toward Travelers Tower, Arun thought the city looked incredible.

Every afternoon after lunch he would walk in the park, sometimes thinking about work, sometimes about life, and sometimes just taking it all in. If he had to describe his mood when he walked, it would be somewhere between happiness and misery. He couldn't tell if it could be attributed to the state of his life or the state of his mind, but it always reminded him of Jimi Hendrix. Apparently, you didn't need drugs to experience a purple haze.

Fall was especially great in the park. Leaves turned, some still on the trees, some already on the ground. Fall colors stood in contrast to the grim and gloomy disposition that he found in himself in his cubicle. He had to change something, his job perhaps, he thought.

Little did he know that his wishes were going to come true. Change would come into his life like a hurricane.

TWENTY

*Two weeks after Sara and
Arun met in the salon*

Arun parked his car and turned to his right. He met her eyes. Sara smiled. "Do you mind waiting here? I will go check to see if they have anything available," he said. She only nodded. He went past the glass doors of the lobby and found the front desk only a few steps away on the left.

"Good afternoon, sir. Welcome to the Residence Inn. How can I help you?" asked a young woman behind the reception desk.

"Any rooms available for today?" Arun asked.

"Let me check sir," she replied, tugging a strand of blond hair behind her ear. "Will it be just for you?" she asked.

"No, it will be for two people." He waited a few seconds and said, "For my . . . eh . . . girlfriend and me."

"No problem. We have a non-smoking King bed available. Will that work for you?"

"I think so," he replied.

The receptionist asked for his driver's license and a credit card. He gave it to her and she got busy typing. After few minutes, she handed him two room keys.

Arun closed the door and turned around to look at Sara, who was standing next to the foot of the bed. The curtains were drawn, so only a faint stream of sunlight passed through them and into the room. He turned the lights on and saw her smiling at him. Her bright white teeth gleamed perfectly between her full, plump lips. Her smooth cheeks glowed in the light, like the way only a young woman's could.

Arun braved a few steps toward her and reached out for her hands. He pulled her closer, their bodies dashing together, their breath flowing into each other's lips. He planted his mouth on hers; a lush, wet kiss. He sucked on her tongue and slowly moved his hands over her shoulders. Her pink Hollister sweatshirt slipped down onto the floor, revealing a half-sleeved blouse with colored circle prints. Arun saw the impression of her aroused nipples through the blouse. He cupped her breasts and kneaded them in a slow rhythmic squeeze, tugging at the tips of her nipples between squeezes. She breathed out a low moan. She closed her eyes and arched her back, her breasts rising toward his mouth.

He unbuttoned her blouse and let it fall to the floor. She wasn't wearing a bra. Arun pushed his head back to behold what was revealed in front of him. Her round, full breasts were climbing higher to reach what they desired. Her pinkish-brown nipples ached and when they were touched again, she gasped for air, sounds of pleasure escaping her gaping mouth.

She shoved her hand into the back of his hair and clenched it tight. Arun pushed her jeans and floral panties down, revealing a thin line of well-trimmed bush. She rested her arms on the foot of the bed to balance herself. He held onto her buttocks and slowly dropped to his knees. His tongue tingled in anticipation.

After some time, he abruptly stood up, looked into her deep brown eyes, pulled her hair back and planted a kiss. He carried her to the bed and laid her on her back. He swiftly removed his clothes and jumped onto the bed with her. Her legs slid apart to accommodate the width of his hips.

TWENTY-ONE

A run offered to drop Sara off at home in the evening. She declined; she would request a Ride-O-Share, she told Arun. He didn't insist. Soon, a ride came. Before climbing in the car, Sara turned and smiled at Arun. She waved at him and Arun saw her lips move, he read "bye." He smiled and waved back. Arun hadn't felt like this in a long time. He hoped she felt the same way.

Arun went back inside the hotel and hung out in the bar a little longer. He watched the Packers beat the Vikings 35-27. Feeling content, he drove back to his apartment. He parked his car in the car port and walked over to the mailbox. There was nothing new. It was Sunday and he remembered that he had checked the mailbox the day before. He opened the door to his building and took a flight of stairs to the second floor. There were four apartments on the second floor, and his was the last one to the left. He keyed in and turned the doorknob to the left. The door opened but only a few inches, as the chain guard stopped it from opening farther. He heard footsteps running toward the door.

TWENTY-TWO

Sunny peeked from the gap between the jamb and the door and squealed, "BABA! MAMA, Baba's here . . . open the door . . . open the door . . ." That was followed by another set of footsteps, these a little heavier and slower than Sunny's. The door closed momentarily, the chain guard clicked, and the door opened fully.

Sunny jumped into Arun's arms and gave him a kiss on his right cheek. Arun reciprocated and put Sunny down on the floor. Sunny ran back to his play table and continued to watch on his Kindle, or *pup pad* as he liked to call it after his favorite Nickelodeon show *Paw Patrol*.

"Hey," Arun said.

"Hi," Ashley replied.

"Who won?" Ashley inquired.

"As usual . . . Packers," Arun said without looking at Ashley.

Ashley went back to sitting on the couch and working on her

laptop.

"Did you eat your dinner?" Arun asked Sunny.

"Yes, I had mac 'n cheese . . ." Sunny replied without taking his eyes off of his *pup pad*.

Arun understood that meant there was nothing else cooked for dinner. He was glad he'd eaten at the bar. He went to the bedroom, changed, came out with his laptop and sat at the dining table. As he turned the laptop on, he looked in front of him. Ashley was sitting on the couch with her laptop; Sunny was sitting on the carpet, across from Ashley, with his *pup pad*; Arun was of course turning his own machine on. The light inside the room suddenly seemed dim. This was his family. He wondered how they'd gotten here.

This was not what he had imagined for himself when he got on the airplane fifteen years ago and came to the United States. But did he have any expectations? Certainly, he thought America would be exotic and he would get to see different things than he was used to seeing in Kathmandu. But Arun couldn't think of any specific expectations he'd had about the new country. He was here to study, finish college in four years, and go back home with an American degree. Surely that would open many doors in Kathmandu. Perhaps that was his expectation, his only expectation.

There were many things in America that fascinated Arun. Trains, for example. Arun loved trains, even though he only saw them during his visits to major cities. Others called it loud and annoying, but Arun found the rhythmic movement of metal clanking on metal as a train traversed through one part of the station to the other soothing. It assured him that there was life in the city. Kathmandu didn't have trains. For that matter, Nepal didn't have trains. He had seen trains only once before, during a family vacation in India when he was five years old. Trains had captured his imagination back then, and Arun was happy to find that they still did.

Trains were exotic, he had told his American friends. They had laughed. They had asked, what was so exotic about the filthy NYC subway? Arun didn't know, but his American friends couldn't change how he felt. What one considered exotic was a matter of what one had experienced before, wasn't it? A lion may not be exotic to a bushman, but to a kid who grew up in Ulaanbaatar, Mongolia, or Worcester, Connecticut, a lion was always going to be exotic. Kathmandu had its share of exotics—never-ending rows of temples and palaces, or the majestic peaks of the Himalayas.

They were exotic to tourists, but not to Arun. What was so exotic about temples and mountains that he saw every day on his way to school? For Arun, trains were exotic, oceans were exotic, and when he came to the United States, he found white women exotic.

Arun wondered why young white women were so obsessed about getting their bodies tanned. What they called tanned was brown in Arun's dictionary. He was already brown, and he did not wish to be browner, thank you very much. He did not hate his skin color; he was only content with what God had gifted him, and he didn't wish to exchange the gift. Arun never understood why so many white women wanted to change how they looked. In his opinion, they looked fantastic. Arun had met plenty of good looking women in Kathmandu, had dated a few already. Like temples and mountains, they were commonplace. But white women were like trains.

And like many men from the west who went to faraway places and married exotic beauties, Arun had married his own exotic beauty, a native Bostonian he had met during his freshman year in college. Ashley hadn't had weight issues back in college. She'd been endowed, no question. But she'd had the right amount of goodness in the right places, as Arun used to put it. She'd gained weight slowly, a few pounds a year. But by the time she had Sunny, the goodness had spread all over her body.

Arun sighed. He looked back at his computer and started typing.

TWENTY-THREE

It was a beautiful spring day. Ample sunshine along with a cool breeze. Sara and Arun spent most of the day at Six Flags. He felt like a college kid again, hopping from one ride to the other. When they got to Superman, he felt queasy; he didn't like the look of it at all. But he didn't say anything to Sara. Whenever he came to the park with Ashley, he always insisted that they try Superman. Ashley would always turn him down. He would tease her and lament that he could not experience the thrill because of her. But deep down he was always relieved when his wife turned the offer down. He didn't have the stomach to handle Superman either.

But now, Arun had no way out. Sara was psyched about this ride, especially because she was finally with someone who matched her enthusiasm. How could he say no? He smiled, faked his excitement. Let her believe what she wanted to, he thought. He was getting pretty good at letting people believe what they wanted to, what he wanted them to.

He got back home around three in the afternoon and took a quick shower. He was in the middle of writing something when he got a call from his wife. He grabbed his dirty-white fedora, put on cologne to mask any lingering smell of Sara, and went out. His wife was sitting in front of Ben & Jerry's with a cup of coffee. *They sell coffee?* He stopped his car and turned the emergency lights on. Ashley opened the door, sat next to him, gave a big smile and a peck on his right cheek. Arun died a little inside.

She was wearing red sweater top and black jeggings. He did not understand the difference between leggings and jeggings, but Ashley had corrected him once when he had called them leggings. Her hair was pulled back into a high pony and her makeup was well blended to match her light skin tone. A pair of stylish purple glasses he had bought for her a year ago elegantly completed her look. He could still see why he had fallen for her.

On their way to pick up their son from daycare, Ashley talked about her day, the fact that she was very hungry, and asked if he would have any problem if they grabbed something quick, Chipotle sounded good to her. Arun had left Six Flags in a rush and hadn't had anything to eat since noon, so he didn't complain either. Normally he would have barked about eating out. In fact, he barked about everything, every day. Today it was one thing, the next day something else. He always barked. Arun felt sorry for Ashley: she had to endure his barking all the time. He parked his car. She climbed out and walked toward the front door of the daycare. He watched her. That reminded him of other times he had watched her walking away from him.

When they had first started dating in college, the basketball court was their hangout spot. Neither he nor she was athletic, but both could throw some hoops. They would chat for hours and hours about this and that. Occasionally, they would play as well. He couldn't remember what they talked about, just that they talked, a lot. If there were more time, they would talk even more. When it was time to leave, Ashley would look at Arun and smile, exactly the way she smiled at him as she walked toward the daycare entrance. They would kiss, and she would walk away. He would watch her hips sway left and then right, in unison with her skirt. It had been more than fifteen years since he had first met her. Her hips no longer swayed like that, but many things were still the same about her. Arun, however, had changed.

Ashley went inside the daycare and the building door closed behind her. Arun's gaze suddenly withdrew from the building door and returned to his car. He saw his face in the rearview mirror, which for some reason was angled toward the driver's seat instead of toward the back of the car. He could not meet his own eyes; he turned away. He held the steering wheel with both hands and closed his eyes. What he had with Sara was the real thing. But Ashley was his wife, mother of his child. It was dawning on him that Sara and Ashley couldn't simultaneously be in his life. He had to let go of someone. If he let Ashley go, Sunny would probably go with her too. Arun couldn't imagine living without his son. More importantly, Arun didn't want his son to grow up without a father. As difficult as it was, a decision had to be made. That day was the last time Arun would ever see Sara again.

TWENTY-FOUR

Once the painful decision was made, the logistics of getting Sara out of his life weren't as difficult as Arun had imagined. He communicated with her via a prepaid cell phone and only through text messages. He had voice and text service, but no data plan. Sara always thought that was odd. *Who in this day and age did not carry a data plan?* she had asked. Arun did not mind her saying that at all; his wife had been saying the same thing for the last two years. He carried an Android phone. No gimmicks, nothing fancy, a cheap smartphone that let him call when he wanted to, text when he needed to, and was Wi-Fi capable. From Arun's perspective, this phone provided all the benefits of a smartphone without the hefty price tag of popular brands like Apple or Samsung.

When he decided to end things with Sara, all he had to do was get a new prepaid number. He thought about meeting with her one last time and ending their relation . . . whatever it was . . . that way. But he didn't know how she would react and thought it would be best to vanish from her life. She worked nearby and though he didn't know where she lived, he guessed it was nearby as well. What if they ran into each other? That he decided he would figure out when it happened. One problem at a time, he told himself. So it was: he ditched his old number and got a new one. He saved his old SIM just in case he needed it in the future. His parents might end up visiting him from Kathmandu and it would be handy to have an extra SIM, he told himself. Not that he would give them the SIM he had used to communicate with Sara. He would give them his new SIM and keep the old one for himself. All of this was hypothetical of course and relied heavily on the assumption that his parents would visit him again.

Arun's parents had come to the US to meet their son and his then-new bride Ashley. By the time they returned to Kathmandu, he was pretty sure they were not coming back. He understood. He didn't blame Ashley or his parents for what had happened. He just understood. It was culture shock, on steroids. He'd grown up with them and although he didn't always believe in their ideas and philosophies, he had learned to respect their opinion. He also understood where Ashley came from; he had known her for most of his adult life and shared lot of her values and beliefs. The same beliefs which were at odds with his parents'. With them, he could let it go; they were his parents after all. Ashley tried to, too, but in the end she couldn't let it go. Long story short, a white American feminist, who also happened to be an atheist, and caramel-colored Hindus of the Himalayas with strong roots in patriarchy couldn't live under the same roof. Although it hadn't been funny when things unraveled, later Arun found the whole episode quite amusing. And people thought opposites attract, he would quip with his wife.

Arun's parents were likely not coming back, but if they did, they would need a phone number, he told himself. He needed some rationale to save the SIM. Arun found out later that National Wireless canceled services of prepaid cards if they weren't used for more than three months. At the time, however, he did not know this, so he saved the SIM card.

TWENTY-FIVE

Just like that, Sara was gone. He went back to his daily life. He continued to work for the insurance company in their Actuarial division. He continued to pick up his son from school and go home. His wife started to come home early and cook dinner; he watched her like he used to when they were in college. She would give him a smile and an expression that said, "Go away, mister." He would go away, play with his son, read him a story, and color with him. Occasionally, he also found time to write. Life got better. Better than it was prior to meeting Sara. Ironically, Sara resuscitated Ashley and Arun's dying marriage.

It had been three years since Arun last went to Six Flags with Sara. Today he was coloring with his son. Sunny was coloring Lookout and Chase and had asked Arun to color Rider, all characters and objects from *Paw Patrol*. Their landline rang, and Arun went to his bedroom to pick up but the cordless was not in the charger. As he was coming out from the bedroom, he noticed that Ashley had already picked up the phone. Arun went back to his son's bedroom and adjusted himself so that he could sit back in his son's not-so-suitable-for-a-grownup chair.

Ashley came over and stood next to him, towering over him. He looked up, gave her a big grin. She was holding the phone in her right hand and was covering the mouthpiece with her left palm. Her hands were covered in flour and so was the phone. She was baking something . . . *Yum, Yum!*

"There is someone on the phone asking for you. Says he wants to talk about Sara Sardana?" Her gestures were non-verbally asking, "What are they talking about?"

Arun felt chills all over his body. Apparently, he did not disguise his expression very well because Ashley immediately asked, "What's wrong? Are you ok?"

He was glad she didn't ask about Sara in that moment. He wouldn't have been able to say anything, but she would have been able to read everything he was thinking through his expression. As his hands moved up to reach for the phone covered in white flour, his mind was tortured by many possible reasons for this phone call. Had someone seen Sara and him and they were now looking to blackmail him? Had she really been underage? He'd had so many chances, why didn't he just look at her ID? Maybe her parents found out and now wanted to cut his head off for deflowering their child? Why now? It had been so long since he had last seen her.

"Hello?" he answered in a muffled voice.

"Is this Mr. Sha? Mr . . . um . . . Aroo . . . Aaron Sha?" said a man in a commanding voice.

"Arun Shah! Yes," Arun replied, trying to sound as normal as he could.

"Mr. Sha, my name is Jim Kelly. I am a detective at the Worcester Police Department. It is my understanding that you are acquainted with Ms. Sarah Sardana. Is this correct?"

It was the worst of all possibilities. Police had found out about his relationship with an underage girl and now wanted to arrest him. Should he plead the fifth now? He thought about telling the cop to get him a lawyer. *Wouldn't I have to be arrested to ask for a lawyer?*

"Mr. Sha, are you still there?"

103

"Yes."

Arun walked over to their guest room and closed the door behind him so that Ashley would not hear his conversation with the cop.

"Are you acquainted with Ms. Sarah Sardana?" the cop asked again.

"It's Sara . . ." Arun replied.

"Excuse me?"

"You were pronouncing her name Sarah . . . but it is more like Saaraa . . . short for Saraswati . . . but she never went by that name." He didn't know why he had to say that. The cop probably already knew.

"What is this about?" Arun asked irritably. His life was getting back to normal and he foresaw it coming to a halt. He blamed the voice on the other end of the line for what was now inevitable.

"Right, Mr. Sha. I think we are talking about the same individual. As you may have heard in the news, Ms. Sardana has been missing for the last thirteen days. We are contacting all her acquaintances to see if they have any knowledge of her. Do you have any information that may help our investigation?"

Arun was dumbfounded. He had just returned last night from a business trip in Hawaii and he hadn't checked the local news yet. He cursed himself for not getting a data plan. Ashley probably knew about the missing woman, but she didn't know who Sara was.

"No. I haven't seen her in years," he replied.

"When was the last time you saw her?"

"Three years ago. We were at Six Flags."

"Did you have any other contact with her after that, text, phone call?"

"No."

"How often did you have contact with her?"

"Probably two or three times a week."

"Is that the number of times you met?"

"Yes."

"And how often did you have other contact? Text, phone call, social media?"

"We only texted and usually to figure out where we would meet. So probably three or four texts a week."

"And what was the exact nature of your relationship with Ms.

Sardana?" the cop asked.

"I beg your pardon?"

"Who was she in relation to you—a friend, schoolmate, colleague, lover . . . what was it?"

Arun was taken aback by the directness of the question. "She was . . . mmm . . . my girlfriend," he answered.

"And who was the young lady who answered the phone?" the cop asked.

Fuck.

"That was my wife," Arun replied.

"And what's her name?"

"Ashley Dupree."

"Were you married when you were in a relationship with Sara?" the cop asked.

"I was," Arun replied.

"I see!" the cop said.

"But we broke up. . ." Arun quickly added. That was a lie. He had broken up with her without telling her. She had never indicated to him that she wanted to end their . . . whatever it was. Arun felt guilty.

"With whom?" the cop asked.

"Sorry?" Arun was confused.

"You said you broke up. I was asking if you broke up with your wife or your girlfriend Sara?" the cop asked.

"Of course, with Sara," Arun said irritably.

"No need to get excited, Mr. Sha. It wasn't clear to me, that's all," the cop said.

There was a brief silence on the other end. "Mr. Sha, we will need to talk more with you. But I cannot do it now. Time is of the essence when we are looking into a missing person case, and I need to contact other folks as well. If anything comes up that you think may help us in the investigation, please call the Worcester PD and ask the operator to transfer you to Jim Kelly. Please leave a message if I am not available and I will get back to you. Now, I would also like you to come by the department tomorrow and give us your formal statement, basically what you told me over the phone. Other investigators may have more questions for you. What time could you come by tomorrow?"

"I can come after work . . ."

"And when would that be?"

"5 PM"

"5 PM works, I will—"

Arun interrupted the cop in mid-sentence: "Could you do 5:30 instead? I take the bus from Hartford and I could only get back to Worcester by 5:30."

"Alright, 5:30 then. I may not be available at that time but will let my partner know you will be coming. When you get here, ask for Jim Kelly or my partner, Sandra Moynihan. Okay?"

"Yes," Arun replied.

"Thanks, Mr. Sha, for your time and we look forward to talking to you soon. Have a good night now."

Arun took the phone off his ear, stared at the screen, and then put it on the end table. He felt alone and scared. He wished he had never met Sara. Then he would not have to explain to strangers who she was or how he knew her or what their . . . whatever . . . was. But all that now looked inevitable. More than anything else, he was afraid of how he would explain all this to his wife.

He was so engulfed in his worries that it took him a good few minutes to realize what he should really have been worried about. Sara. She had been missing for thirteen days and the cops didn't seem to have any leads whatsoever. If they did, their next priority item would not be to contact someone she had last seen three years ago. That much he could put together. He decided he would tell the cop everything. He wasn't sure how that would help in finding her, but there was certainly no point in holding anything back now.

But before that, he needed to come clean with Ashley.

TWENTY-SIX

November 2016

Gabriel was in Katie's room. It was the same room he had visited many times in his dreams. Today was no different. A blur of white light on the ceiling and Katie's shape in front of him. She was wearing the same dress she always wore. After a while, Gabriel thought it suited her well, especially the black hem. It matched the black blur she had on her head, her hair. Her expression hadn't changed either. He couldn't see her facial features, so he couldn't identify whether her expression had changed, of course. But he could sense the energy in the room. It was dull and dreary. The same energy he always felt in his many dream visits to Katie's room.

Today they sat in silence. Not uncommon for Katie, since she never initiated their dream conversations. But it was unusual for Gabriel to not say anything. He looked at Katie, then looked down at the bed he was sitting on. He saw the blur of his legs; he moved his toe. A few light bubbles moved, just like a pixel in a monitor. But Gabriel wouldn't know, he did not know what a pixel was. He wanted to talk to Katie, but what should he talk about? Was he running out of topics? Or had he caught whatever melancholy disease Katie had?

Maybe it was time for him to say goodbye to Katie and start dreaming about something else. He was about to say something when a pixel in the top left quadrant of his vision moved. He looked up to bring the moving pixel into the center of his field of vision. Katie was looking at him. He rubbed his eyes and looked at her again. Yes, he thought, she was looking directly at him. He shook his head vigorously from left to right, as if that would make him see more clearly. It did not. But . . . but it was clear she was looking at him. His blurred pixels didn't lie, not even in a dream. Katie was certainly looking directly at him.

"Katie?" Gabriel said.

No answer.

"Katie, you are looking at me, aren't you?"

No answer.

"Say something please, Katie?"

"What do you want?" The blurred figure spoke curtly.

Before Gabriel could reply, the blurred figure spoke again, "What do you want, you prick?"

There was coldness in the voice, and did he notice a . . .

Gabriel didn't say anything. Katie had never spoken to him in that voice before. True, she wasn't the same anymore. Dream Katie wasn't as warm as the real one, but she had never been mean to him either. Dream Katie's attitude toward Gabriel had been more indifferent than angry.

"WHAT DO YOU WANT?" The voice was getting louder and louder.

WHAT DO YOU WANT?

WHAT DO YOU WANT?

WHAT DO YOU WANT?

The pixels started to move all over the place and the blur moved toward him. He closed his eyes, but he could not close his ears.

She screamed at the top of her lungs.

"YOU WANT TO FUCK ME, YOU PRICK? ISN'T THAT WHAT YOU WANT TO DO? TALK TO ME, YOU BASTARD. DO YOU WANT TO FUCK ME? FUCK ME THEN. FUCK ME. WHY DON'T YOU FUCK ME? FUCK ME. HERE."

The voice stopped abruptly. Gabriel heard weird noises and the pixels continued to move all over the place, but his brain was flooded with too many things to decipher anything. He closed his eyes; he was breathing heavily, his heart beating faster. He closed his ears with his palms. He screamed. "WAKE UP. WAKE UP. WAKE UP."

The last thing he heard, as it all started to fade away was, "FUCK ME. LOOK. FUCK ME. HERE."

TWENTY-SEVEN

August 2016

Jim finished his call with Arun and walked over to Sandra's office. He knocked once; she looked up.

"He was sleeping with her . . . and the guy is married," Jim said, leaning against the doorjamb.

Sandra raised her brow and slowly bobbed her head. Jim filled her in on the conversion he'd had with Arun Shah. Sandra pushed her chair back and walked over to the whiteboard on the wall. There were a dozen names on the whiteboard, and nine of them had been crossed off. The last three names were Ross Anderson, Sara's boyfriend; Vitaly Kolmogorov, a Ride-O-Share driver; and Chuck Lagano, a customer at Charming Lady. Sandra picked up a black dry-erase marker and wrote Arun Shah below Chuck Lagano, Ashley Dupree below Arun Shah.

She turned and looked at Jim. "Let's hope we get something out of these two," Sandra said, pointing to the new additions on the whiteboard.

Jim frowned. "Well, he says he hasn't seen her in three years. Says he was in Hawaii for the last few weeks. We will see about that tomorrow, but I am not too hopeful about this one, Sandy. I didn't even bother going to meet him, called him to the station for a statement instead. What happened to the other three?" Jim said, pointing to the whiteboard.

"Well, I interviewed Chuck. Like you thought, he is one weird guy."

Jim smirked.

Sandra continued, "At first he wouldn't admit that he knew Sara, but once we talked about CCTV footage, he caved in. He had all sorts of red flags—inconsistent story, backtracking, and most interestingly, the amount of narcotics we found in his caa—"

"Car?" Jim interrupted. "You already got a search warrant?"

"Chuck helped." Sandra grinned.

"Well, sounds like significant progress, maybe I should have stayed sick."

"I didn't want you to worry. Thought you would rest better if you didn't get constant updates from us." Sandra flushed.

Jim waved his hand in air. "You're fine. But do tell," Jim said.

"I showed his interview footage to the D.A. and that was all she needed. Like I said, something looked wrong about that guy. First, he wouldn't admit to knowing Sara. Then he reluctantly admitted that he knew her from the Charming Lady store where he went to buy something for his wife. I asked him what that 'something' was and he said he couldn't remember. You know about the bikini stuff."

Jim nodded.

"He then walked to the checkout counter and met Sara. He claims Sara told him he was her last customer that day and she was going to call her boyfriend to pick her up after she signed out. He didn't say anything to her then, but after she checked him out, he called her to the side and offered her a ride in his car instead. He claims Sara took the offer and said she would be right out. She asked him to wait for her in his car. He slipped a sticky note in her hand with his number just in case she was unable to locate him in the parking lot. He then went out and waited for about twenty minutes. When she didn't come, he drove back to his house."

"Do you believe him?" Jim asked.

"Oh! I don't know, but there are things that do add up." Sandra said.

"Like?" Jim asked.

"Well, there is no way to confirm if Sara told him about her plan to call her boyfriend after work. We know from Ross and his cell phone provider that she had indeed called him, but Chuck could have easily read that in a newspaper as well. By the time we interviewed Chuck, the whole fiasco between Ross and Sara's parents had already unraveled . . . but the CCTV footage from inside the store did show that he pulled her to the side, talked to her, and slipped a note—consistent with what he told us."

"So what? It still sounds promising to me," Jim said.

"Well, that's what I thought too, and like I said, getting a search warrant from the D.A. was easy enough after we showed her his interview footage as well as interview footage of other store employees. The problem was, we didn't find anything in his car or his house. Nothing belonging to Sara, no DNA. Well, I should rather say lots of DNA but nothing of Sara. Oh, and he is now lawyered up. Unless there is a significant development that points us toward him, we are not going to hear from him again."

"How do you feel?" Jim asked.

Sandra shrugged. "He is either clean or really good at cleaning."

Jim looked down on the floor, knitting his brow.

Sandra went back to her desk, sat, and leaned back in her chair.

"The CCTV also showed that Sara exited from the front door of the store. He was parked at the rear parking lot and exited through the back door. So, if you strictly go by the data we have on him, there is nothing to go further on, but the fact that Sara vanished after talking to an A-class perv makes it more unsettling," Sandra said.

There was silence in the room.

"He could have taken her somewhere else, not his house," Jim said.

"Sure," Sandra said, "Certainly could have. But he would've had to take her there somehow. His car already came up negative, like I said. Even if you think there was another car or accomplice involved, we will need to find either the car or the accomplice first. The guy does not have to talk anymore since the search has cleared him from the DA's perspective. Like I said, something new must point us in his direction if we are going to pursue him again. Based on what we have, he is all done."

Jim contemplated what Sandra said and then asked, "What

narcotics were you talking about?"

"Oh, yeah, almost forgot about that. He had this whole stash of painkillers, some in his car and some at home. Apparently, all legitimately prescribed. His lawyer provided the prescription and just dismissed it as irrelevant to the investigation because he could stash his prescription medication however he wished. But those painkillers were not your everyday stuff, you know. They were strong. More than capable of knocking someone out cold," Sandra said, cocking her left eyebrow.

Jim nodded.

There was silence again.

"Any new developments on the other two?" Jim asked.

Sandra shook her head. "Nothing new. The Russian guy does not say much, other than *yes* and *no*, as you know."

Jim nodded.

"Ride-O-Share is backing him up since they don't have any record of Sara's ride request either. They are claiming he just happened to be parked in the shopping center parking lot, waiting for a ride request from potential customers."

Sandra rounded her arms behind her head and continued, "Ross has been cooperative, but we still haven't received an alibi for the crucial three hours from the time Sara disappeared to when he showed up at the storefront looking for her. He has records of making phone calls to her parents and a few of her friends that he knew of. He waited twenty-four hours and then reported her missing. Things you would want to do if you didn't want to come across as a suspect."

"Very cynical," Jim said.

Sandra jerked forward. "All I'm saying is that I would feel a lot better about him if he had an alibi for the first three hours. Between 3:30 PM and 6:25 PM he says he was in his apartment watching football and waiting for Sara to come home. When she didn't pick up her phone and didn't show up, he left for the Greenmile Walk shopping center. Even though it was Sunday and the shopping center closed at 6 PM, the store employees were still inside the store finishing up for the day. Well, that's his story, at least."

"The store manager and other employees did confirm his story though," Jim said.

"Only the part after he showed up at their door. Not the story about what he did between 3:30 PM and 6:25 PM. In fact, nobody saw him on Sunday before 6:25. All we have is what Ross told us: he was home, watching football. If you ask me, Chuck is now looking in much better shape than Ross."

Jim sighed. "What now, Sandy?"

Sandra smiled and said, "Well, hope your new guy and his wife have something to add to the puzzle. Maybe something happened three years ago . . . or maybe this guy is lying about their last meeting being three years ago. The wife has even bigger motivation to see Sara disappear. Husband's mistress is always unsavory, whether present or ex-."

Jim nodded and sighed again. He stood upright, tapped twice on the doorjamb, turned around and left. Sandra went back to looking at her computer.

TWENTY-EIGHT

A run typed *Worcester PD, Connecticut* into Google and saved the address in his cell phone. At the carport, he typed the address into the GPS and drove out. Even though he had lived in Worcester for the last five years, he realized that he had never been to the part of the town where the police department was. He technically lived in the town of Worcester, but for all practical purposes, he really lived in the neighboring town of South Hampton, where Sara had lived with her boyfriend. Arun's apartment was very close to the neighboring town, he did all his shopping in South Hampton, and Sunny went to daycare in South Hampton, too. Until today, Arun had never had a need to go to the other side of Worcester, the old town.

In the parking lot of the Worchester PD, there was a large pole with an American flag at full mast. The building was red brick, something he didn't see every day in Worcester or South Hampton. Everything these days seemed to be made from vinyl siding or as his dad would put it, "plastic."

He opened the glass door and approached a female officer sitting behind the desk. He said he was looking for Jim Kelly. He paused to look for a sticky note in his pocket. He pulled it out, looked at it, and added, "Or his partner Sandra?" The officer asked what this was about and Arun said Jim Kelly wanted to talk to him about the Sara Sardana missing person case. The officer gave a nod and asked him to sit in the waiting area.

After a few minutes, a tall and burly gentleman opened a door and came toward Arun. He had grey-black hair and a matching moustache. His hair was combed all the way back. He was certainly a big man, but not fat, Arun couldn't see a paunch. Jim introduced himself, shook Arun's hand, and asked him to follow him inside.

Jim took Arun to a room that resembled an interrogation room like Arun had seen in movies. Jim probably saw concern in Arun's eyes because he said, "Don't worry, this should be quick. We want the statement you gave me yesterday and to see if you have any other information that can help us with the investigation. Time is running out for us and for Sara and there is nothing called bad information at this time. I need to leave the room to get my partner, I will be back soon." Jim shut the door behind him.

In few minutes, Jim returned with a female companion, who looked like she belonged more in the chair Arun was sitting in rather than in the aisle across from him. She had parted her hair; the left side of her part was cut very short, but the right side of her hair fell all the way to her shoulder. Her hair was dyed jet black, she was wearing wine colored lipstick, a skull necklace, a black leather jacket, and leather pants. Her expression was somewhere between indifference and passive rage. Arun immediately felt hatred directed at him.

Jim introduced her as Sandra Moynihan. Both Jim and Sandra sat across from Arun: Jim directly in front of him and Sandra to Jim's right. Jim put on his reading glasses and looked at a piece of paper. He said, "Mr. Sha?" He pushed his reading glasses to the tip of his nose, looked up at Arun, and added, "Did I say your name correctly this time?"

"Yes," Arun replied curtly. It was his first name the cop had mispronounced the previous night, not his last name. Arun kept quiet.

"I am turning this recorder on. Why don't you start from the very beginning, with how you met Sara to the last time you talked to her."

Arun obliged and told his story of finding Sara in the middle of what might have been his mid-life crisis. Jim asked a lot of follow-ups. Sandra just stared at Arun. Jim asked about places they had visited together, the number of sexual encounters they'd had, whether they'd had any fights, etc. When Jim finally announced that was all for the day, Arun was relieved and stood up to head out. Jim took out his reading glasses, put them on the table, and said, "One more thing, Mr. Sha. Did you know how old she was when you first met her?"

Arun shook his head. His heart throbbed.

"She disappeared one day after her 21st birthday. You met her about three years ago, you said? Well, I will let you do the math. In any case, finding her is our priority right now more than anything else and you have documented proof that you were in Hawaii when she disappeared . . . so . . . please stay close by until the investigation is complete. You are one of the very few people who knew Sara closely. We may want to speak with you again. If you can avoid any travel outside of the state, that would be better. If you absolutely need to travel, please let us know first. Have a good day, Mr. Sha."

Arun nodded and left. He left the building as fast as he could. He checked his watch and couldn't believe he'd been inside that room for more than two hours. No wonder he had felt like he was suffocating. At least now there was nothing left to hide. Last night with Ashley and today with the police, opening about his relationship with Sara had felt cathartic. He finally felt comfortable calling it a relationship. Yes, it was a relationship. A relationship filled with love and respect. A relationship that had nothing to do with anyone's age or country of origin or race or ethnicity. A relationship they both had cared for and adored. A relationship that Arun had abandoned. A relationship he had betrayed.

Arun wondered sadly if his abrupt departure from her life had anything to do with her disappearance. A long time had passed since his betrayal . . . he hoped . . . he prayed . . .

TWENTY-NINE

November 2016

Three months after he first drove to the Worchester PD, Arun was driving to the police station again. He tried to understand what he was feeling. Quantitatively, this emotion was familiar. He was queasy and groggy, his heart was beating faster, waves of energy traversed through his body. It could've been anything—anger, anxiety, fear, even happiness. But there was something qualitative about this feeling, too. That quality told him precisely what it was—guilt. He looked at the box on the passenger seat one more time. It was definitely guilt. He parked his car. The American flag in front of the station was waving gracefully in the wind.

The officer sitting behind the front desk told him Sandra Moynihan was out of office and Jim Kelly was in a conference room. She asked him to wait in the lobby until Detective Kelly became available.

Arun was not planning to wait. This was important, something Jim needed to know yesterday. Arun saw an officer walk toward a locked door.

From his past visit, he knew that all of the conference rooms were inside the door. He followed the officer, who scanned his ID card on the access control reader. The door opened. The receptionist complained from behind the front desk. That made the officer at the door turn toward the front desk. He was much taller than Arun and a paunch jutted over the top of his pants.

Arun ducked under the officer's arm and sidled inside the door. Before the officer realized what had happened, Arun had already rocketed toward the conference area. He heard footsteps behind him and yelling directed at him. He opened the first door on his left and was immediately relieved to see a familiar face. Just as the door opened, a couple of cops who had been running behind him came crashing into him and pinned him to the floor, face first. His head went numb, his chest tightened, and he felt suffocated. He heard a mumbled discussion, and soon he could breathe again. Someone must have asked them to let go of him.

His ears were still ringing as he struggled to get up. He dabbed his forefinger under his nostrils and looked. His vision was all blurred, but he could tell the color was red. Someone grabbed him by his arm and helped him up. He rubbed his eyes. The haze slowly cleared, and he saw Jim Kelly, arms akimbo, looking furiously at him.

"You need to be glad that one of our men didn't shoot you. What the fuck is going on now, Arun?" Jim said.

"I . . ." Arun swallowed blood and sputum. "I . . . speak with you?"

"That much I figured out as soon as I saw you. But I hope you understand that others wouldn't know that. Don't you ever do . . ." Jim stopped himself, waved his hand in the air and said, "I don't think there is any point in telling you anything. Just remember that next time you do what you just did, don't blame us for a bullet in your head. You understand?"

Arun nodded.

"I want you to say that you understand." Jim was almost shouting.

"I understand," Arun said, mustering enough energy.

"Go on," Jim said, lowering his voice this time.

Arun tried to catch his breath. He looked around the room and then looked back at Jim. He said, "In person?"

Jim Kelly looked around and nodded to the rest of the officers. Slowly the conference room started emptying out. When the last person had left and closed the door, Jim offered Arun a seat. Jim walked all the way across the table, grabbed a chair, rested his clasped hands on the back of the chair, and waited. Jim did not sit. He said, "You have five minutes."

THIRTY

This is about Sara," Arun said.

Jim sighed and spoke slowly, enunciating every word carefully. "Mr. Shah, we have discussed this many times. In our line of work, when someone has been missing for this long, ninety-three days to be precise, and we don't have any leads, we start to consider this a cold case. This is hard for you, I understand. But we have already cleared you out as a suspect and you don't need to do anything to exonerate yourself."

"No, but I do. I do." Arun raised his voice and hammered his fist on the table. Jim raised his eyebrows, folded his arms, and stood upright. The door behind Arun opened and an officer peeked in. Jim waved. The door closed.

"I am sorry, but . . . look . . . hear me out . . . okay?" Arun continued, this time in a softer tone, "This guilt, this guilt, I need to get it out."

Jim didn't say anything. He just looked sternly at Arun.

"You need to look at this." Arun reached into the inner pocket of his jacket and produced a plastic box and pushed it toward Jim.

Jim's brow furrowed; his outstretched hands reluctantly held the box up. It was a transparent plastic box that could be used to keep and protect something small. Jim opened the box and gave Arun a quizzical look as he pulled out a mobile SIM card. Jim pinched it between his right index finger and thumb and asked, "What is this?"

"It is a SIM card," Arun replied.

"I know this is a SIM card, Arun," Jim said irritably. "What do I do with this?"

"I will show you," said Arun and signaled Jim to pass the SIM card.

Jim obliged. Arun took out his phone from his pocket, flipped it back, opened the battery cover, and took out the SIM. He grabbed the other SIM from Jim and inserted it into his phone. Once the phone was turned back on, he clicked on voicemail. He turned the speaker on and handed the phone back to Jim.

"You have seventeen messages. First message . . ." the automated voice said.

"Skip to the last one . . . keep pressing seven to skip," Arun said to Jim, then hesitated for a moment. "Perhaps I should do it." Arun took the phone back in his hand. He pressed seven sixteen times and put the phone back on the table. "Next message," said the automated female voice.

What could be heard of the last voicemail was muffled, as if something was covering the mouth piece. Intermittently, the sound would get clearer and you could hear a woman screaming Arun's name. The sound would dim out again and then a few seconds later the same woman's cries would grow louder again. There was a struggle; she was trying to fight back. Finally, a sound of shattering glass, then the automated voice said, "No further messages. To go back to main menu . . ." With misty eyes, Arun grabbed the phone and pressed cancel.

When Jim didn't say anything, Arun said, "That was Sara . . . I mean is . . . I hope she is still . . ."

"When did you get this message?" asked Jim.

"Must have been when she vanished . . . or before she vanished," replied Arun.

"How come you are bringing this to me now? Why didn't you tell us you had this message when we interviewed you?" asked Jim, furrowing his brow.

"Because I didn't know I had this message," replied Arun.

Jim put both palms on the conference table and said, "That doesn't make sense, Mr. Shah. This is clearly your voicemail. How come you didn't know you had a voicemail for this long?"

Arun sighed. Looked down for a moment.

"Answer me, Mr. Shah," said Jim.

Arun looked up and said, "Look Jim, I am here because I found this voicemail and wanted to share it with you, in the hopes that it could help with the investigation. But I am sensing an accusatory tone in your voice and I don't like that one bit. If I had anything to do with Sara's disappearance then I wouldn't be stupid enough to walk into your conference room, get a beating, and then show you something that would incriminate me."

After a brief silence, Jim said, "I am not accusing you of anything, Mr. Shah, but a revelation like this after so long amounts to a possible charge of withholding evidence. You deliberately withheld valuable information which may have been helpful in our investigation had we known before. After more than three months, I don't know what to do with this information."

"I wasn't withholding anything, Jim. I just found this yesterday and came to tell you right away," replied Arun.

"I don't understand what you mean. You didn't check your voicemail for three months?" asked Jim.

"I did check my voicemail, but this is not my voicemail . . . at least not a regular one," replied Arun.

"You'll need to elaborate, Mr. Shah. This isn't making any sense to me," said Jim.

"I carry a prepaid phone, Jim." Arun explained why he'd a prepaid phone and why he'd decided to the save the SIM after getting a new number.

"A few weeks ago, I was looking for some documents in my office and found this small box with my old SIM. I thought about Sara immediately and on a whim put the old SIM back into my phone. I didn't get any service from *National Wireless,* but the voicemail icon flashed with the number '17.' I clicked on the voicemail, but it errored out. I called

National Wireless and asked them what was going on. The customer service folks were not able to figure it out, so they created a ticket and sent it to their technical help department. I have been calling them every day since. They kept making excuses for why they couldn't do anything about these voicemails since my service had been canceled almost three years ago. I told them I wouldn't have it any other way, I needed these messages no matter who I needed to talk to. Basically, I pestered and pestered. They forwarded my calls to their higher ups. At one point, I was talking to the vice president of customer relations. I think that did the trick finally . . ."

Jim sighed and glanced at his wrist watch momentarily.

"I got a call back from their technical help yesterday . . ." For the next several minutes, Arun described in detail what the technical help at National Wireless told him.

"Since this option was selected rarely, *National Wireless* hadn't encountered this issue before . . ."

"You got your voicemail back. Mr. Sha, I got it," Jim finally interrupted, drawing in slow breath.

"Well, yes . . . Sorry, I thought you'd want details . . . anyway, when I put the SIM back in the phone, the voicemail app connected to my webmail and recognized that I had seventeen unread messages. *National Wireless* told me they're going to fix this glitch, but before they did, they were able to retrieve my voicemails and make it available in my phone. I also asked them to reactivate my old number, and they reluctantly did. I was told that I shouldn't expect any of this going forward. That was fine by me. I listened to the messages and all were from Sara; all were from three years ago, except for the last one. In most of the messages, she was wondering where I was. She was worried about me, she thought something may have happened to me since I wasn't picking up the phone. On the sixteenth message, she sobbingly said she'd found out about my marriage. If I wanted her out of my life, all I had to do was ask, she said. The seventeenth message . . . well, you know about that one."

Jim removed his hands from the conference table, stood upright, turned around, and took a couple of steps toward a TV monitor behind the conference table. Behind the TV monitor was a glass wall. The conference room had one glass wall and the rest of the three walls were opaque. Through the glass wall, Arun could see a few officers looking inside with interest. Jim stood in front of the TV monitor, facing away from Arun, staring vacantly into the glass wall.

"Do you know what this means, Jim?" Arun asked.

Jim turned his head around, his body still facing the glass wall.

"It means that as Sara fought for her life, she turned to me for help. Me, the guy who wanted to get her out of my life. She still thought I was the guy who could help. Even after three years. Not her good-for-nothing boyfriend, not her parents or friends, but me. And . . . and . . . she paid the price . . ."

Arun choked up. "I won't be able to rid myself of this guilt, Jim."

Jim walked across to the other end of the conference table. He put his hand on Arun's shoulder and said, "Don't beat yourself up too much, Arun. You did the right thing bringing this to us. I don't know how much of this is going to be of help at this time, but I am going to keep this with me if that is okay with you."

Arun nodded.

"We will see what we can do. This at least tells us that she was in a place where a glass could shatter. Maybe a house, maybe a warehouse . . . but not a car. It sounded more like a glass dropping on the floor rather than a broken window, you know?"

Arun nodded.

"This could also mean that she may have voluntarily gone to this warehouse or house, only then realizing something was amiss and calling you. That would explain why nobody at Greenmile Walk noticed anything unusual. Whether she took a Ride-O-Share or rode in another car, she might have left Greenmile Walk willingly. Maybe with someone she knew." Saying this, Jim outstretched his hand. Arun took out the SIM card from his phone and put it in Jim's hand.

"I am going to be right back, please stay here, okay?" Jim went out and closed the door behind him.

THIRTY-ONE

Arun put his arms on the table and buried his head in them. Guilt pulsed from his heart through his whole body. After some time, he opened his eyes, lifted his head up. He touched his forehead; it was damp. A trickle of drool glazed the side of his chin. Had he dozed off? His mouth still had a metallic taste. He dabbed under his nostrils again; the blood had dried.

He walked to the other end of the conference table to see if he could use the TV as a mirror. He could make out the shape of his face but couldn't see anything in detail. He was about to head back to his chair when he noticed a pile of CDs inside a cabinet, under the TV. The cabinet door was ajar. There were five CDs in the pile. The label on the topmost CD read, "George Buckley." He couldn't see the labels for the rest. But one of the CDs in the middle was sticking out slightly from the pile. Arun could read only the first two letters on the label "Sa . . ." Arun pushed the cabinet door open

and pulled out the middle CD to get a better read.
Sara Sardana: Amigo's Mexican Grill.

Outside the conference room, Jim Kelly was talking to his team about Arun's story. There was a consensus among his team that they should interview a few people again now that they had new information, especially those who were close to Sara, those with whom Sara wouldn't have been threatened to ride in a car with. Jim listened to his team and nodded in agreement, but there was something in Arun's story that bothered him. He couldn't pinpoint what it was, but something didn't add up. He was an instinctive person and his instincts told him he was missing something.

He looked into the conference room and noticed that Arun was right in front of him, inside the glass wall of course, but in front of him. But he wasn't looking at Jim. Instead, his head tilted to the right and his eyes were fixed on something below Jim's waistline. Jim self-consciously touched his fly. He looked at himself and the rest of the team and noticed nothing unusual that would have invited such concentration. Then he noticed the TV. Jim fumed. He made a few quick steps toward the conference room and jerked the door open.

"I DID NOT AUTHORIZE YOU TO START USING OUR EQUIPMENT MR. SHA." The conference room boomed with Jim's voice and so did the hallway outside. "I WILL HAVE TO ASK YOU TO TURN THAT OFF IMMEDIATELY AND WALK OUTSIDE THE ROOM."

Arun turned around. For a guy who'd seemed like he would burst out wailing seconds before Jim had stepped out of the conference room, Arun looked unusually calm now. "This is the CCTV footage from the store . . . across the street from Charming Lady," Arun said cheerfully, jabbing at the TV screen.

"I know what that is, Mr. Shah, but that is not something for you to look at. It is for Police Department use only," said Jim, still furious.

Arun raised both hands as if Jim was pointing a gun at him. "What did the driver from the . . . uh . . . that . . . stopped car . . . say?" Before Jim could answer, Arun added, "I don't know what to call that car . . . more like parked-in-the-middle-of-the-road car? What did you guys call it?" Arun's cheerfulness had been replaced by serious curiosity.

Jim was about to boom again, but he stopped himself. He looked at the TV screen, looked back at Arun, and said, "What the fuck are you talking about now?"

Arun didn't say anything. But his expression said it all. His small eyes ballooned, his brows climbed as high as they could.

"Don't tell me you don't know about the car that is stopped in the middle of that road in the video?" Arun pointed at the TV screen and watched Jim in horror.

Jim stood still and just stared at Arun.

Arun slumped his head, shook it a few times, and raised it back to face Jim.

"Jim, I think you should hear me out . . . I know you have every good reason to toss me out of here . . . sorry, I shouldn't have put this CD on the player or barged in like a lunatic earlier. I am sorry, Jim . . . I really am. So, I can totally understand that you want me out of this conference room, but please know that I only mean to help. Don't look at my actions . . . consider my intentions," Arun pleaded.

Jim remained silent and continued to stare at him. But Jim's expression must have told Arun that he had calmed down.

"Why don't you please sit down?" Arun pulled out a chair, placed it in front of the TV, and patted the seat.

Jim hesitantly obliged. He didn't admit it to himself, but he was curious too.

"I saw Sara's name on this CD and I couldn't help it. My apologies again . . . for not asking for your permission. Look at all the cars on the video going in the opposite direction. From your earlier reaction, I am guessing that you and your team haven't paid attention to these cars moving in the opposite direction. Is this true?"

"No, that is not true. We have paid attention to everything on that tape. The reason we haven't looked at cars moving in the opposite direction is because there are no goddamn cars moving in the opposite direction," Jim said, pointing at the video. "On top of the screen cars are moving from right to left and at the bottom of the screen cars are moving from left to the right. That is what it's supposed to look like in CCTV footage. All the cars are in their correct lanes. No cars are moving in the opposite direction." Jim had just finished saying this when the conference room door opened.

"What is going on here?" asked Sandra.

THIRTY-TWO

Sandra Moynihan had just stepped inside the police department when the receptionist informed her about the situation. Jim looked at Sandra and said, "Nothing, Sandy. Mr. Shah is clearly delusional and probably hasn't slept well in the last couple of months. He is also this close to getting thrown in jail." Jim brought his right hand close to his face, and pinched his index finger and thumb very near, without touching.

"Ms. Moynihan, could you please take a seat as well. I think I am onto something here," said Arun. "Please hear me out. Based on Jim's reaction, I think we may have missed something in this video. Something crucial in my opinion, but you can decide after you hear what I have to say."

Sandra looked at Jim, who shrugged and gave her a "don't ask me" look. She grabbed a chair and sat next to Jim.

"All right, Jim, you are right. What you explained is correct . . . well partially correct," said Arun.

Jim shifted in the chair.

Arun continued, "The cars on top of the screen are moving in the correct lanes. As seen on CCTV, from the right of the screen to the left of the screen. No question about that: we are on the same page. But if you look at the cars on the bottom of the screen, they only appear to be moving in the correct lanes, from the left side of the screen to the right side of the screen."

"What do you mean by *appear*?" Sandra interjected, throwing air quotes. She continued, "The cars on the bottom of the screen are also moving in their correct lanes, Arun. Otherwise it would look like two-lane one-way traffic."

"That is why *appear* is the key word and perhaps why we missed it . . . you guys missed it, sorry," Arun said.

Jim looked irritable and said, "You will have to explain fast what you are talking about, Arun, before I throw you out of the building."

"If you continue to look, you will see that all the cars on the top of the screen, the ones moving from the right to the left, do not touch the doubled-lined yellow divider in the middle of the road. Do you see that?" Arun said, raising his eyebrows and leaning in toward Jim and Sandra.

Sandra nodded but Jim only stared at Arun.

"Okay. Now look at the cars that are coming from the left of the screen and going toward the right. Can you say the same thing about these cars?" asked Arun.

Both Jim and Sandra squinted their eyes. Sandra was the first to answer, "I cannot see whether or not they are touching the yellow divider line. The camera angle is from the bottom of the screen. The bodies of the vehicles are blocking the divider line."

"That is correct but look at the back of this car . . ." Arun jabbed his finger on the TV. "It is ever so slightly tilted up instead of being parallel to the road. That suggests to me that it must be touching the yellow line," declared Arun triumphantly.

"What the fuck is this?" Jim bawled. "Whether it is touching yellow line or not, what does this have to do with anything? Stop wasting our time, Mr. Sha, and get some rest. Looks like you need some." Jim stood up.

"Hold on, hold on. Give me a minute." Arun cautiously moved toward Jim, waving both hands rhythmically in an up and down motion, trying to convince Jim to stay where he was. "I will prove to you that it is relevant. Please, Jim."

"Get out of this building on your own, Mr. Shan, before we have to drag you out."

"Please, Jim . . ." Arun said.

Jim grabbed Arun's left arm and pulled him toward the door.

Arun tried unsuccessfully to resist Jim and kept pleading.

"I will prove to you that if these cars are indeed touching the yellow lane divider, then Sara must have climbed inside one of the cars—"

Jim stopped.

"And I may be able to identify the car itself. I cannot clearly see the license plate number of the cars on this footage, but once I point out the car to you, you must have some way to zoom in on the license plate?"

Jim looked at Sandra. No reaction. He looked at Arun then back at Sandra. This time she shrugged. Jim let go of his grip on Arun's arm. Arun put his right hand over on his left arm and rubbed. He moved back toward the TV. Jim hesitantly sat down again.

"Ms. Moyni . . . er . . . Sandra, you were right. I can only hypothesize that based on the tilt of the cars they may be touching the yellow lane divider. I cannot prove it 100%. Is there a recording from another angle that we can look at?"

"We could show him the Charming Lady footage?" Sandra suggested, turning toward Jim.

THIRTY-THREE

Charming Lady was a women's clothing store located among the Promenade shops at Greenmile Walk, where Sara had worked as a sales associate. On July 31st, she had clocked out and walked across the street to a burrito joint, Amigo's Mexican Grill. She had stayed there for exactly 15 minutes and 22 seconds. She'd come out of the burrito joint and turned to her left. Arun and the two cops had been watching the CCTV footage from the burrito joint. There was also CCTV footage that police had obtained from the Charming Lady.

Jim gave Sandra a stern look.

"Might as well, Jim. It's been a while now and we have no leads. If anything can come out of this, it's worth a shot," Sandra said with a shrug.

Jim didn't say anything. Sandra got up and walked over to the TV stand. She looked at the pile of four CDs Arun had discovered. After not finding what she was looking for, she scanned her card on a small card reader located on the handle of the adjacent cabinet. She shuffled through CDs and came out holding one. Sandra handed it to Arun and walked back to her seat.

"Would you ask Janet to be careful with the cabinet locks next time?" said Jim to Sandra. "We shouldn't be this careless with investigation materials, you know?" Jim pointed to the now fully open cabinet where Arun had found the first CD.

Sandra nodded.

Arun appeared flushed. He jerked away, put the CD in the player and waited patiently. It was the CCTV footage from Charming Lady. At the top of the screen was Amigo's Mexican Grill. Just below the stores was a sidewalk, then roadside parking, and below the parking lot was the street. Amigo's was the corner store on the other side; Charming Lady was the corner store on this side. Arun matched the clocks on the two CCTV footage segments, so that they could look at the same cars from both angles. Arun scanned the CD to 3:33 PM, a few minutes before Sara had walked out of view in the CCTV footage from Amigo's.

Watching the CCTV footage from the Charming Lady, they could see Sara at the top of the screen, coming out of Amigo's. She stood on the edge of the sidewalk, just in front of Amigo's. On her right shoulder was a brown handbag. She took out her phone, spent some time looking at it, then put it over her ear. After what looked like a brief conversation with someone, she took her phone out of her ear. She looked at the phone again, for a little longer this time, and put it in her brown handbag. Her boyfriend had confirmed that after coming out of Charming Lady, she had called him to ask if he was going to pick her up. He had asked if she could share a ride instead and she had replied that she could. So far, the stories lined up.

Looking at the CCTV footage, police had also believed that the person Sara was talking to was indeed her boyfriend. They had matched the time on his call log to the time recorded on the CCTV. After hanging up her phone, the time she spent looking at her phone again was believed to be for calling a Ride-O-Share ride. This however could not be confirmed. Ride-O-Share claimed that there were no ride requests made from her phone on July 31st.

After she put her phone in her handbag, she could be seen folding her arms for a few minutes and waiting on the sidewalk in front of Amigo's. She turned right and then left. Then she could be seen walking over to her left. She quickly glanced over her shoulder. Police had looked at hours and hours of footage from other stores to see what Sara might have been looking at. They had interviewed a few people too, but nothing was conclusive. Sara then walked beyond the field of view of the camera. The time was 3:39 PM.

That was Sara's last known location. That was ninety-three days earlier.

Since both Amigo's and Charming Lady were corner stores, no other CCTV camera covered the section of the shopping center where Sara went. About a hundred yards away in the same direction Sara had walked was the New Marine Store. But New Marine was too far away for its CCTV to cover this stretch of the shopping center. Sara had walked into a CCTV blind spot.

Jim, Sandra, and Arun watched Sara vanish into the right side of the TV screen. Arun reminded everyone that since they were now looking at the footage from the Charming Lady store, they were trying to see if cars at the top of the screen, coming from the right side of the screen and going to the left side of the screen, were touching the yellow double-lined lane divider.

Sandra was quick to point out that the cars moving from the right side to the left were mostly moving inside the yellow divider line. Arun didn't say much but kept looking at the video. By 3:40 PM, an increasing number of cars were touching the divider line with their back tires. It was difficult to say exactly when this pattern had stopped, but by 3:45 PM, it was gone completely and the cars coming from the right side of the screen were moving inside the yellow line.

Arun looked at Jim and Sandra, his eyes now wide.

THIRTY-FOUR

Jim was the first to speak. "This does not prove anything, Mr. Shah. So what if some cars crossed over the line or were on the line. Maybe they were just bad drivers."

"It does not bother you that all the bad drivers in the world suddenly converged at Worchester Greenmile Walk shopping center somewhere between 3:40 and 3:45, and by 3:45 these so called 'bad drivers' were gone again?" Arun asked.

"It is curious all right, but how will this help our investigation?" Sandra asked.

"It may or may not help, but I have a theory that I want to discuss with you guys," Arun waited for Sandra and Jim to say something. When they didn't, Arun continued.

"We have established at this time that something unusual happened in the traffic pattern between 3:40 PM and 3:45 PM. Suddenly,

100% of the cars coming from the right side of the screen started touching the yellow lane divider, the same side Sara was last seen walking toward. No such pattern was seen on the other side of the road. Cars going from the left to the right of the screen seem to stop and go but they stay inside the yellow divider line. Even if we consider this a completely random event, that suddenly bad drivers converged at the shopping center at the same time, I find it hard to digest that this random phenomenon only affected one side of the road . . .

"Instead, I think there is a good explanation for why this happened. Jim, imagine for a second that you were driving a car in that shopping center and suddenly a car in front of you stopped. If it were a two-way traffic, double-lane road just like we see in the video, what would you do?"

"I would wait for the car to move," Jim replied.

"Okay. How long would you wait before deciding to honk?" Arun asked.

"Don't know. Maybe 10 to 15 seconds. Well, it would depend as well. If there was a traffic jam, I could just wait and not honk," Jim replied.

"That is a good point," said Arun, nodding his head. "I should have pointed out that there was no traffic jam. The car in front of you just stopped. There was no jam in front of the car. Let me also add that no other cars are coming from the other side. You have pretty much an empty road and only the car in front of you has decided to abruptly stop. How long would you wait before honking?" Arun asked.

Jim thought for a while and then said, "If that is the case then I might not even honk. You said no cars are coming from the other side, correct?" Jim asked.

Arun nodded.

"I would just pass it over."

"And how would you do that?" Arun asked.

"How would I do what?"

"How would you pass this car?"

"You don't know how to pass a car, Mr. Shah?" Jim replied irritably. "Go over to the other lane, pass this car, and get back to my lane."

Arun pointed his index finger accusingly at Jim, "A minute ago, you were calling all those folks who had their back tires barely on the yellow line bad drivers, and now you are willing to completely cross over to the other lane?" Arun smirked.

Seeing Jim getting flushed, Arun quickly changed his tone. "All right, so that is my exact point. What Jim said. My hypothesis is that a car must have stopped in the same direction that Sara was seen walking toward. The car must have stopped far enough from CCTV's field of view that the cars behind the stopped car had enough time to cross over to the other lane and come back to their correct lane. Fortunately, the CCTV cameras captured the back tires in the act of crossing over to their correct lane. At this point it may be redundant to say this but I will say it anyway: I think Sara climbed in that stopped car. Based on Jim's earlier deduction from the voicemail, she climbed in willingly, without force. Maybe with someone she knew well enough."

Sandra looked at Jim, and then back at Arun. "What voicemail?"

Jim filled in Sandra on what she had missed.

There was silence in the room. Jim and Sandra looked at each other. Jim spoke first, "This is completely within the realm of possibility, Mr. Sha, I will give you that. But how would we know which one was the stopped car? We have looked at this video many times to identify any passengers that looked like Sara and we did not find any. There were quite a few cars with tinted windows, which makes it impossible to identify people inside. We even interviewed quite a few drivers. For all I know, your stopped car could have taken a U-turn and headed out the other way. In any case, even if what you are saying is true, I don't see how this will help us locate Sara."

Arun sighed. He looked at the floor.

Sandra spoke. "If you extend your crossing-the-yellow-line theory a little further, we may be able to locate the car."

Arun and Jim didn't understand. She looked at Arun and said, "You said that the fact that 100% of the cars touched the yellow lane divider sometime between 3:40 PM and 3:45 PM wasn't a mere coincidence or a statistical anomaly. But rather an effect of a proper cause, a stopped car. If so, then when you remove the cause, the effect should go away as well."

Arun and Jim were still concentrating on Sandra's face, but she didn't see the comprehension she was looking for. "Follow the cars that exhibit anomaly, and then when the anomaly stops, the first car that is completely inside the yellow line should be your stopped car. Of course, this is not perfect since the driver of the stopped car could actually be a bad driver. In that case, he or she could have crossed the yellow lane divider as well. Another situation is what Jim mentioned—if the car made a U-turn then the first car inside the yellow lane divider would be a false positive."

"But something worth investigating, right?" Arun asked jubilantly.

"I suppose," Sandra said and looked at Jim, who stiffened his upper lip and nodded very slightly.

"Good. Besides, I think the U-turn theory is implausible given how narrow that stretch of the road is. You would have to make a U-turn in backed up traffic that you caused, further backing up the traffic on both sides of the road. You would be much better off driving straight ahead," Arun announced.

M.K. Shivakoti

PART TWO

THIRTY-FIVE

August 2016

Roman Bland had been anxiously waiting for Michael Carter, Roman's lawyer and a good friend. Roman answered the door and the men exchanged a warm greeting.

"What brings me over here, Roman?" asked Michael.

Michael Carter was one of the very few people who was allowed to call Roman by his first name. Roman had left a voicemail on Michael's cell phone citing an "urgent matter which needed to be dealt with yesterday."

"Why don't we sit first. I am going to order breakfast for two of us. Hope you haven't had anything yet?" asked Roman.

"No."

"The usual then?"

"Yes, that will be fine," replied Michael.

"While I am on the phone, why don't you grab that Hartford Courant on the chair and read the article I circled on the front page?" said

Roman, pointing at the chair.

Michael removed the newspaper and sat on the chair. The cover story was of the presidential election. The cover photo was two separate pictures combined into one. Donald Trump was pointing his index finger at Hillary Clinton, who was behind the dais on what looked like one of her campaign trails. "Post-Fed announcement Trump campaign gains momentum, Clinton camp in panic," read the headline. To the right side of the election story was a small section with a headline circled in blue ink. "Police baffled over missing South Hampton woman. Third day, no lead." Michael had just finished reading the piece when he realized that Roman had been looking over his shoulder, standing quietly.

"What is this?" asked Michael.

"What do you think?"

"About the missing woman?"

"Yes."

"There is nothing to think about. I cancelled my morning appointments to be here. Please don't tell me you invited me to chit chat about a missing woman," replied Michael, looking up at Roman, who was still standing.

Roman sat across from Michael and said, "This is not just any missing case, Michael. This girl was one of our employees . . . well, non-employee technically—a contractor—but she worked across the street in our main building."

"And?" Michael tilted his head and raised his eyebrows, inviting Roman to explain more. When Roman didn't add anything, Michael scoffed. "Clearly you cannot be concerned about a missing contractor?"

"Ex . . ." replied Roman.

"What?"

"Ex-contractor."

"Even better, an ex-contractor of the company is missing . . . so?"

There was a knock on the door. A butler entered with breakfast. A chicken fajita omelet for Roman and a breakfast sampler with two pieces of ham, two slices of bacon, hash browns, and scrambled eggs for Michael. Roman suggested that they eat first. Michael nodded. Both ate breakfast in silence.

After a few minutes, Michael said, "Look, I have known you for a long time. Unless this was significant, you wouldn't have asked me to come this early, knowing that I would have to cancel my other appointments. So, can you please cut to the chase and tell me what's going on?"

Roman nodded and started speaking as he poured coffee on the mug. "Her name didn't mean anything to me, but as soon as I looked at her face in the newspaper this morning, I recognized who she was. I met her at the company's diversity event. I was the chief guest and had given a talk about empowerment. There was a social hour after the talk and light refreshments were served. This girl, Sara Sardana per the newspaper, came by and introduced herself. There was a small group gathered around me and we were making small talk. But soon the number of people started to dwindle and for a few brief minutes, only two of us were left. I asked her how she liked her work and she replied that she loved her work and could see herself doing it for a long time. But she explained it was also tough, given the temporary nature of her employment. She then asked if I could spend a few minutes listening to her situation and offer any advice or feedback. I told her I indeed had a few minutes and would be happy to listen to her situation. She said since her situation pertained to work, she would feel uncomfortable discussing such a matter in public. Somebody could just stop by. She wondered if I could lend half an hour of my time to guide her. I told her that would be fine and asked her to come over to my suite at the Marriott if that worked for her. She said that would work, and then we shook hands and parted ways."

"Why didn't you ask her to meet with you during normal work hours . . . in your office?" asked Michael with a frown.

"I don't know. If I am really honest with myself I think I know why. But at the time I told myself that she looked like she was in distress and it was only for half an hour anyway. Besides, she was just asking for advice."

"Nobody is just asking for advice, Roman. You have worked long enough to understand that. I already don't like the sound of where this is going, but please continue."

"Anyway, I came back to my suite, and ordered my dinner. I had just finished eating when I got a call from reception informing me that Sara was here to see me. She came up, a butler was still in the room when she entered. She sat where you are sitting right now."

"Before you go any further, please tell me you have nothing to do with her disappearance."

"Well . . ."

"Roman, the answer should be no, an emphatic no. It should always be no. Never start with well . . . unless you actually did it."

"I did not, okay! But I do think I may have played a role in pushing her . . . I don't know. That is why I have you here today. But you have to hear me out first . . ."

Michael sighed. "Go ahead."

"Where was I?"

"I think you were saying she sat where I am sitting."

"Oh yes. She started to talk about her temporary status and how she would like an opportunity to apply for a permanent role. Long story short, she wanted me to intervene and help her find a permanent role as soon as possible. At first, I wasn't keen on doing anything but the more I listened, I was drawn to her soft manner, personality and by God, those legs. It feels absurd now but at the time it seemed like a perfect opportunity for a deal. I will help you out, why don't you do the same. And so it happened . . .

"Next week, I reached out to her management to fulfill my side of the agreement, but found out she had turned in her resignation earlier in the week and no longer worked for us. I told them I was following up as her mentor, I don't think they thought anything else. That was it. I didn't hear back from her and she was quickly out of my mind until I read the paper this morning."

Michael closed his eyes and took a deep breath. "This is some awful shit you got yourself into, Roman," Michael fumed.

"Despite discussing these matters with you so many times, I cannot believe you . . . I have worked like a pimp for you and that wasn't enough?" Michael turned his head to his right and shook his head in disbelief. "You are not just my employer but my friend as well, Roman, and I hope you realize what a lousy situation this puts me in . . . puts the *company* in. This is exactly why we started this personal secretary shit, to avoid situations like this."

Roman didn't say anything. Michael had been a good friend and Roman understood his frustration. Before Michael had come into the suite, Roman had felt the same way about himself.

"Should we talk to the police?" asked Roman.

"Right, and then we call a press conference, don't we?" said

Michael scathingly. "No police, no statement, nothing for now. I will prep my team on how to respond if someone contacts us but nothing until they come to us. Do you hear me? Nothing until they come to us?"

"Yes," Roman obliged.

"How many people did you say saw her coming over to your whore house?" asked Michael nonchalantly.

Roman shot him a look. There was a clear boundary on how to talk to Roman Bland, even for Michael Carter.

Michael waved his right hand apologetically and said, "Sorry, how many people do you think saw her?"

"The receptionist and the butler. I don't think anyone else would have," replied Roman.

Michael bobbed his head up and down. "That should be ok. They have probably seen enough women coming in and out of here to not be alarmed. They should know your reputation by now. How long ago was this?"

"Thre—a few months back . . . I don't remember exactly."

"Do you remember the names of the butler or the receptionist?" asked Michael.

Roman shook his head.

"That's fine. I can talk to the hotel management and figure it out. I will check to see if there was a log of this girl's visit as well."

Michael thought for a minute, looked up at Roman, and asked, "You do understand what I am concerned about, don't you, Bland?"

Roman hesitated for a minute and said, "I think so. The woman I had sex with is missing?"

"Not really, that was months ago. But even though you are not involved in daily operations of the company anymore, you are still the chairman. Hence, she was your employee. The problem is that you had sex with your employee."

He continued, "You topped that by offering her permanent employment in return. I am pretty sure that would be illegal even in the most fucked up country in the world."

"I did not offer her permanent employment," Roman shot back.

"What did you offer then?"

"That I could try to help, but it was her choice."

"What was her choice?"

"Well . . . okay, I . . . okay."

Both men sat in silence. Michael spoke first.

"Focus on your work for now and try not to think about it. What you did can't be undone. I will look into a few things on my end and will keep an eye on where things are with the police investigation. They may not even care about all this from what I can tell. Like you said, you last saw her months ago and the police would be most interested in finding out where she is now rather than who she fucked a few months ago. If they do find out that a person like you had sex with her, they may want to understand if you had a motive to make her disappear. You would look very suspicious to them because you fit the profile of someone who has money and power to make people disappear forever. Moreover, it will be bad press for us and a whole lot of legal trouble for you. These are not exactly ideal times for powerful men who take advantage of less powerful women . . . unless you are the President."

Roman smirked.

"Since you are not, it is better for you to stay put and observe. Just hope that she stays disappeared so your little adventure does not come into the light. Unlike other women you've fooled around with, she did not sign any non-disclosure agreement . . . You understand?" Michael asked.

Roman nodded.

Michael stood up, shook Roman's hand, and left the suite.

Roman closed the door after Michael and went over to the chair where Michael had left the courant. Roman picked up the newspaper one more time. He looked at the face smiling at him. He'd made the right decision, he thought. There were things that even your own lawyer shouldn't know. At least not now.

Roman put the newspaper down on the coffee table and went into the bathroom to take a shower.

There was one more magazine on the coffee table. The July issue of *Time* magazine had Roman Bland's picture on the cover page. The cover title read, "BOARD MEMBER DESCRIBES NEW DIRECTION FOR RIDE-O-SHARE."

THIRTY-SIX

November 2016

Sandra Moynihan was still fiddling with a cigarette when Jim said, "Don't smoke in my car please . . . I thought you quit?"

"I did," Sandra replied.

"Then what is that?"

"I quit smoking, I can still hold the cigarette." She looked at him and gave a half smile.

"What is cooking in that little head of yours, Sandy?"

"You can tell I'm thinking?"

"Yeah . . . and what was that staring competition about? Besides, you hardly spoke, asked what, three questions?"

"Two, to be exact," Sandra replied casually. "You know how I can tell whether someone is guilty or not?"

"How?"

"I look into their eyes the whole time we are interviewing. Most of the time, you are interviewing, and I am looking . . . or staring, the way you put it. I think you learn a lot about a person when you look into their eyes. What do they say? Bridge to the soul?"

"Eyes are mirrors of your soul," Jim corrected.

"Yes. That. I 100% believe in that. For the last ten years I've been interviewing people, or while others have interviewed people, I've looked into their soul and I've never been disappointed. Their soul always tells me the truth, regardless of what the person is saying. Once I know the truth, I either move on to another suspect or I just have to find the evidence. But . . ."

"Sounds like the woman's soul disappointed you this time, Sandy." Jim laughed.

"Not disappointed. But if eyes are mirrors of your soul then her soul must be empty. I saw nothing. It was dark and vacant."

Sandra continued, "I come out of these interviews with a pretty good idea of what to do next. For the first time, I am not sure."

"We will have to double check her story if possible, but from what I could tell, it checks out, Sandy, wouldn't you say? She didn't know what we knew about the stopped car. But she told the story unsolicited and it matched everything we knew."

When Sandra said nothing, Jim continued. "Granted her story didn't match Arun's hypothesis, but the story that the woman shared was good. No holes."

"Maybe too good," Sandra said.

"You don't believe she was telling the truth?" Jim asked.

"I don't know, Jim. I wish there was a way to corroborate her story through an independent source. Her husband will most certainly repeat every single word that came out of her mouth, and it's just her luck that where she stopped the car was a CCTV blind spot. I don't think New Marine's CCTV footage would cover that section either. It's her story versus . . . Arun's hypothesis. And I hated her smirks and those excited eyes. What the fuck was that all about? We are trying to find a missing girl here." Sandra sighed and gave Jim a dejected look.

"I think you are thinking too much, Sandy. I didn't like her either. Seemed too friendly and nice. I don't trust people who appear too friendly. In my experience, they are the ones who will cut you into pieces when nobody's watching. I'm gonna go to New Marine at Greenmile Walk and see if they can give me CCTV footage from July 31st so that we can verify parts of her story."

"It's already November, I doubt they will have footage from more than three months back," replied Sandra.

"That's what I am afraid of too, but we've got to try something. Do you want to come with me?"

"Nah! I don't think you will get far with New Marine footage, even if they have the footage. Drop me at the office. I want to talk to the lab folks again and see if they can give me more license plate numbers."

Jim frowned, puzzled. "For what? She just confirmed that her husband's car was the stopped car."

"Arun's hypothesis was that Sara climbed inside the stopped car. I just want to talk to other drivers who were blocked by the stopped car to see if they can give me an independent account of what transpired. Maybe they will tell me something that she was not saying. If the window was open and they were really barking at each other, then I think someone would have noticed something. Besides, maybe the lab will find Ashley's car in the vicinity as well," Sandra said.

"You still think Ashley could—"

Sandra interrupted and said, "Why, because she is a woman?"

"Wow . . . wow . . . slow down, missy." Jim held up his hands. "I know what women are capable of all right, both good and bad stuff. But I don't see Ashley being able to carry out such a . . . First, she is . . . well, a big woman—"

Sandra interrupted again and said, "Oh, I get it now, so because she is a fat woman . . . nice going, Jim!"

Jim sighed. "You have to let me complete my thoughts, Sandy! I will just say that I can't see her doing this. Besides, we have nothing to point us in her direction."

"Well . . . I won't say nothing. It's more than curious in my opinion that she left early from work on July 31st, the same day her husband's mistress disappeared," Sandra said.

"Ex-mistress, Sandy. Besides, she didn't even know about their affair until Sara disappeared," Jim said.

"Bullshit! How do you know she didn't know?" Sandra asked.

"Because she said so," Jim replied.

"Ha . . . you have been doing this much longer than I have, Jim.

Start sounding like a cop," Sandra said.

Jim didn't say anything.

"How do you know she isn't lying? Arun texted with Sara; she could have easily read his messages," Sandra said.

"Then why keep quiet about the affair for so long? Why now?" Jim asked.

There was silence in the car. Sandra was the first to speak. "If she really wanted revenge then maybe she was looking for the right opportunity. Maybe she was planning . . . but honestly Jim, I don't know. I hope I can find something to prove that she was lying. A workaholic who hadn't missed a day of work in three years tells her boss she isn't feeling well and leaves early on the same day her husband's mistress disappears. She wasn't even supposed to be at work. It was Sunday, it was her day off. But she came in, showed her face to everyone, so that they could confirm that they had seen her that day, and then left. This has to be more than just a coincidence. She left work at 3:00 PM, which her management confirmed. But we have no way to confirm what she did after that. She claims she went home and slept. Arun was away in Hawaii and their son was at his grandparents' house in Boston. Her management saw her the next day at 8 AM. They said, and I quote, *She looked so refreshed the next day,*" Sandra said.

"It's not a crime to look refreshed, Sandy," Jim said.

"Maybe she looked refreshed because she got her sweet revenge . . . Anyway, that is speculation, but the fact is that nobody saw her between 3:00 PM on July 31st and 8:00 AM on August 1st. It's a 15-minute drive from her work to the shopping center at the Greenmile Walk. Sara was last seen at 3:39 PM on CCTV."

Jim didn't say anything. They both sat in silence the rest of the way to the police department.

THIRTY-SEVEN

November 2016

Today was Arun's third day in the hospital. Over the course of his stay, many different doctors had visited him, usually repeating questions or asking very similar ones. All evaluations, mental and physical, had come back normal. His heartbeat had been slightly irregular yesterday and he continued to have low blood pressure. The doctors wanted to observe him a little. He could potentially go home this evening. They had tried to wean him off of the pain medication but as soon as it was stopped, all the thoughts came rushing back: Sara, his inadequate life, his unsuccessful marriage. He asked them to turn the pain medication back on. Everything was peaceful again, no more thoughts.

He heard a knock on the door. It was Ann Horowitz. She came in and held the door open. She kept looking outside the door instead of looking at Arun. She finally looked at Arun and said with a smile, "You have a visitor."

Arun's eyes brightened up and he immediately thought, *Sara!* They must have found her. He waited patiently with giddy excitement. A bald young man entered the room carrying a white cane.

Ann spoke first. "Arun, I would like you to meet Gabriel. He is our special care specialist. He heard that you haven't had any visitors yet, so he wanted to come visit you and talk to you. Would that be ok?"

Arun was disappointed but he nodded. Ann helped Gabriel to a chair, smiled at Arun, and left the room, closing the door behind her.

THIRTY-EIGHT

A run looked at the young man and thought he must be handicapped, maybe blind? Come to think of it, Arun had never met a blind person before. He had seen them in movies or occasionally out on the streets, but he couldn't recall having had a single conversation with a blind person. Arun looked at the young man again. He didn't see any deformity in Gabriel's eyes. Blind people have peculiar eyes, don't they? Like milky eyes, or constantly moving eyes, or sunglasses, or something. Usually you could tell if someone was blind by just looking, couldn't you? The only indication of blindness Arun saw in Gabriel was the cane. Gabriel looked pensive and hadn't looked at Arun yet. He was staring down at the floor and rotating the white cane slowly. For several minutes, they stayed silent. Arun was the first to speak.

"Ann said you wanted to talk to me. What did you want to talk about?" As soon as he finished asking this, Arun noticed another sign of blindness. Gabriel looked toward Arun, reacting to Arun's voice. But Gabriel wasn't looking at him directly. His head was moving left and right ever so slightly as if scanning for Arun's exact position. Arun bent his body to the right; Gabriel's eyes followed him. Arun sat back straight. Gabriel's eyes followed him back. Arun was confused.

"I am sad today. Sorry, I am usually very talkative. My name is Gabriel. I'm a boy. Your name is Arun, right?"

Before Arun could reply, Gabriel continued, "Ann told me you did not have anyone under emergency contact either. Is that true?"

Arun said that was true. Not because he did not have any family or friends but because he had been through rough times lately and wanted to be alone. He did not want to bother his friends and family. If they knew he was in a hospital, they would be obligated to visit him, and he did not want that. He did not want to force anyone to do anything for him. These last couple of days in the hospital had been peaceful for him and he wanted to cherish it as long as it lasted. Later, at an appropriate time, he would let them know.

Gabriel nodded. "I understand," he said and fell silent again.

Arun was again the first to speak. "You said you were sad today. May I ask why?"

Gabriel said he was afraid he might have lost his best friend. Not lost as in died, but as in did not want to be his friend anymore. In fact, it seemed like his best friend might now turn into his worst nightmare, literally speaking.

THIRTY-NINE

Arun understood losing a friend. He had married his best friend who now no longer wanted to live with him. Arun couldn't understand how he'd gotten himself into this situation. Until very recently, his life was a perfect example of what it was supposed to be like. Arun had been a straight "A" student throughout school, finished college in four years, finished graduate school in another two, and then landed a very good-paying job. He was married to the love of his life and together they created a beautiful child. Everything that anyone could hope for, the envy of the world. Yet, an unexplainable void existed in his heart. *Ungrateful is what it is*, Arun sometimes lamented. He should have been more grateful for what he had instead of wishing for something else. Wishing that he didn't have to force himself to go to work every day. Wishing there was something more meaningful than calculating how much insurance premium to charge a customer.

Arun tried hard to convince himself that his job was meaningful. After all, insurance was an important industry. He himself had benefited from insurance in his personal life. A couple of times when he'd had car accidents, the total cost of damages had exceeded $15,000. But his out of pocket expense was only $500. When Ashley's mother went through cancer treatment, the total cost easily exceeded $50,000 annually. But out of pocket expense for a year was only $6000. All because of good insurance. He was appreciative of the insurance he carried and felt a sense of pride for being part of the industry that helped people during difficult times. But the initial high of working in insurance, at a Fortune 100 company, and getting paid a handsome salary had worn off after a few years. The grim reality then set in: for the next thirty-five years, Arun's work would consist of the dreary ritual of following a peculiar insurance cycle of growth versus profitability.

In that regard, Arun had a relatively easy job. He knew exactly what to expect each cycle and what his manager and their manager and their manager . . . expected. That was another absurdity. There was a never-ending number of managers and the hierarchical organization meant very slow progress. It also meant an easy job. Just show up at work, keep smiling, and plug away based on the strategy for the cycle. Not hard, right?

Arun was furious at himself. Why couldn't he just do that? Why did he have to look for "meaningful work?" He knew that the elusive "meaningful work" would not pay for health insurance, make a dollar-for-dollar matching contribution to his 401k, and definitely would not pay a six-figure salary. So why look for one? He had a child to look after and plenty of bills to pay. It made no practical sense. Whatever the reason might have been, he couldn't help himself. His productivity had deteriorated and that had impacted his personal life as well. He hadn't been able to find "meaningful work," but he had managed to screw up his already meaningful family life.

"I am sorry about your friend, Gabriel!" Arun said. "You said your best friend could be your worst enemy now. If you don't mind me asking, what happened?"

"I don't know if she is now my enemy or not, but I don't think I want to be in front of her anymore. I am afraid of her," Gabriel said, tears welling up in his eyes.

"Your best friend is a girl?" Arun asked.

"Was, remember? Past tense," Gabriel said. "Her name is Katie." Gabriel told Arun how he met Katie at Mercy Hospital, how they bonded, and why she left the hospital. He also told Arun about life after Katie and his humdrum existence at Gamma and Pa's house. For a moment, Gabriel's eyes gleamed when he mentioned that she had come back into his life. This time in his dreams, not as a real person. That joyous expression lasted only briefly, substituted by horror when he recalled his last dream, two days ago. Katie had since stopped coming into his dreams, which surprised Gabriel, but he was equally relieved. He hoped she would continue to stay out of his dreams for good.

Arun didn't interrupt Gabriel, just listened to him. When Gabriel started to explain his dreams, it became obvious to Arun what had happened. Katie's abrupt departure must have had such an impact on Gabriel that his brain had compensated by recreating her in his mind. He wasn't a psychiatrist, but anyone could deduce that much. The only thing Arun didn't understand was why Gabriel's brain had created such a dark and melancholy Katie, when everything he had known about Katie in real life had been like rainbows and unicorns. He didn't say anything to Gabriel. He thought he would ask Ann after Gabriel left.

"I am glad you aren't dreaming about her anymore, Gabriel. That did sound awful and scary," Arun consoled. "Why are you sad then? Shouldn't you be happy?"

"No. I can't be. I miss her. I looked forward to seeing her. Before that bad dream, that is. I still love her very much and it saddens me that the last memory I have of her is her screaming at me and getting mad. And all those bad words she said to me?" Gabriel shook his head in disbelief. "Why? I know what those words mean, you know. I am no dummy. Pa uses them all the time at home and I asked one of my friends at school. I know it's a bad word and a bad thing. Why did she think I would do that to her? To my best friend?"

Arun knew a lot of people who would do the same "bad thing" to their best friend. He was one of them. But Arun knew that Katie wasn't talking about making love when she was screaming YOU WANT TO FUCK ME, YOU PRICK? There was something sinister. You don't scream FUCK ME with murderous rage when you are looking for it. Arun wondered what awful monster resided in Gabriel's poor mind.

FORTY

abriel stayed in Arun's room for two hours. They ate ice cream together and then Gabriel got a message that his Gamma was waiting for him in the hospital lobby. As Gabriel exited the room, Arun raised his index finger to get Ann's attention. When Ann looked his way, he moved his index finger to his lips and immediately curled his fingers to indicate *come here*. Ann looked outside the door and said, "I can come with you to the lobby if you want, Gabriel?"

From his bed, Arun heard a faint voice, "I got it, Ann. I made many trips down to the lobby from this floor. Every Wednesday and Thursday, remember?" She closed the door behind her and came closer to Arun with a look on her face that seemed to say *wooo gossip!*

"What is his story?" Arun asked.

"Why? He didn't tell you?" Ann looked at her watch. "He was here for more than two hours!" she said with a smile.

"Well, I know everything about his imaginary friend but nothing about him. I didn't feel comfortable asking him about his medical condition and things like that, you know."

"He suffers from a birth defect, I think, that's why he is blind. More like partially blind. He says he can see shapes and colors, night and day, but cannot read or write. You will be amazed by how well he can recognize people, though. He won't tell us how he does it but we all think it's a sensory enhancement."

Arun furrowed his brow.

Ann continued, "All that means is his other senses—smell, touch, hearing, taste—probably work better than ours. Happens all the time with disabled folks. Nature has some way of compensating for what has been taken away."

"What about his parents?" Arun asked. "He talked about his grandparents with me and I think his grandmother was in the lobby to pick him up. He never mentioned his parents."

"I have also only talked to his grandmother because she is the one who comes to pick him up. I haven't asked his grandmother anything personal like that, but Gabriel told me that he lives with his grandparents and his mother died a few days after his birth. Some postpartum complication according to his imaginary friend when she was not very imaginary," replied Ann with a grin.

"What about his dad?" Arun asked.

"Don't know. He never talks about his dad and I have never asked," Ann replied.

"This Katie girl. You say she wasn't imaginary. How do you know? Have you met her before?" asked Arun.

"I haven't met her, but I asked his grandmother once out of concern for his mental health and she confirmed that there was a volunteer at Mercy Hospital that Gabriel had befriended. Apparently, she found a paid gig somewhere in the city, and then left the volunteer job. It seems she didn't tell Gabriel and left without meeting with him," Ann replied.

"What did his grandmother say about his mental state?" Arun asked.

"She said they consulted a psychiatrist and that there wasn't any clear diagnosis. Katie appears only in his dreams and it is not like hallucination or something, you know. No medication for a recurring dream." Ann was grinning again. "His grandmother has asked us to keep an eye on him so that she can update his psychiatrist about Gabriel's status. As far as we are concerned, he is all normal. Besides, look at what he does for us? And for you. A minute before he was in this room, you were like a lifeless body and look at you now, asking away these questions with all that curiosity in your eyes." Ann winked and laughed.

Arun laughed as well. It had been a while since he had laughed genuinely.

"You can talk to his grandmother if you want," Ann said. "She will be able to tell you more. His grandmother is a nurse at Mercy Hospital as well. Really sweet lady. If we keep you here today, you can ask her tomorrow when she picks him up."

FORTY-ONE

They didn't keep Arun in the hospital that long though. He was discharged Wednesday evening. Hoping that he could still meet with Gabriel's grandmother, Arun drove to Mercy Hospital the next day. Arun had nothing else to do. Ashley had said she couldn't live with him anymore knowing he'd cheated on her. She had taken Sunny with her. His mental health had become so delicate that his employer gladly put him on Family Medical Leave of Absence. He had no job, no family, and no lead in Sara's case. So, Mercy Hospital it was.

He entered the main building and walked toward the security desk on the left side of the lobby. To the woman behind the desk, he asked if he could meet with one of the ICU nurses, Rose Galligan. The security lady asked him what this was about. Arun told her about Gabriel and how he had helped Arun while he was at the Worcester Memorial Hospital with a head injury. Arun only wanted to share his gratitude with Rose, wanted to know a little more about her grandchild and if there was anything he could do for Gabriel.

This was true. Arun was curious about Gabriel but there was also a sincere desire to help. Since Sara's disappearance, Arun's life had turned upside down. He mostly stayed in his apartment by himself, depressed, his wife and son long gone, his career finished, his ambition non-existent, living like a degenerate. He had started to contemplate whether he should even bother to keep living. Binge-watching TV and porn did not feel like life's purpose. Gabriel had sparked something in him.

He didn't explain all of this to the security woman, but she must have understood the gist of it. She kept looking at her screen and said *un-huh, un-huh*, nodding her head at regular interval. Finally, she looked up at Arun and asked for his photo ID. After a few minutes, a printer buzzed and soon she handed him a visitor's badge. She pointed to a corner behind him, slightly to his right, and spoke slowly, as if explaining to an elementary school kid. "Take the elevator to the fourth floor, that's the ICU. Go to the nurses' station." Her eyes moved past him. "Next in line," she announced loudly. Arun's eardrums complained.

He took the elevator to the fourth floor and passed through the automatic glass door. Straight in front of him was the nurses' station. "Hi, my name is Arun Shah. I am looking for Rose Galligar?"

The woman sitting behind the desk was middle-aged with a pixie cut, and looked like a strict headmistress behind Harry Potter glasses. She clasped her hands together, resting them on the desk in front of her, and said, "Are you asking me or telling me?"

Arun wasn't sure. "Sorry?"

"Why do you need to see Rose?" asked the woman in a raspy voice.

He repeated one more time what he had told the security woman earlier. Unlike the security woman, the nurse smiled and said, "How nice of you to come by, all the way from Worcester!" The tone of her voice had changed, and she sounded friendlier. Mercy Hospital was only a fifteen-minute drive from his Worcester apartment and it was no big deal to Arun; he was happy to have something to do that wasn't his usual ritual. But the woman behind the desk didn't need to know that. Let her believe that he'd "come all the way." He gave her a fake smile.

The woman spoke again and said, "Rose took a day off today, I am actually filling in for her. You can check back tomorrow . . . maybe." Her

M.K. Shivakoti

fingers curled up, shoulders raised, eyebrows cocked; she wasn't sure.

Arun sighed and then nodded.

"Call us before you come over though, so that you don't have to drive all the way from Worcester if she is not around."

He nodded again. "Thank you very much," he said. He was about to turn around when a thought flicked through his mind. He paused.

"Did you know Katie by any chance?"

She gave him a broad smile and said, "You know, if I had any doubt that you had actually met Gabriel, that question alone would have erased it all. I sure know Katie. Not very well, she volunteered for a short time a few months ago. I never met her in person either, but just like yourself, anyone who knows Gabriel knows Katie."

Arun's eyes brightened up. He looked at his watch, it was 11:30 AM. "If it is not too much trouble, can I talk to you for a few minutes about Katie and Gabriel? I don't want to impose and certainly don't want to keep you away from your work. If you are taking a lunch break or coffee break anytime soon, I just want to chat for a few minutes, that's all."

"Well, I don't mind at all, but we don't have designated breaks in our profession, you know. When it's not busy, that's when we take a break. And it is always busy." The woman rolled her eyes. She looked at her wristwatch and said, "I will probably go down to the cafeteria in another fifteen minutes, but it could be two hours too, you know."

"That is fine, I can wait. I've downloaded a book on my phone, so take as much time as you need. I will wait at the cafeteria," Arun said.

"Outside the cafeteria there is a nice courtyard with stone benches. If you are going to read, the weather is nice, and you might as well sit outside," she said with a smile.

"Sure, will do. Thanks again . . . Ms . . ."

"Caroline Heathers," replied the woman, offering her hand.

Arun shook her hand and said, "Thank you, Ms. Heathers."

"Just Caroline."

"Thanks, Caroline. I will see you soon then."

FORTY-TWO

Caroline arrived after an hour with a lunch box. "Sorry, like I said we never know how long it will take." She shrugged.

"No worries. I made good progress," Arun replied, jabbing at the phone screen.

She took her seat across from Arun and looked at the iPhone 5S he was holding. "Isn't that small for reading?" she inquired.

"Well, you can increase the font size and make it as large as in a hard copy book. The only downside might be that you flip pages too often. That hasn't bothered me, but might bother others," he replied. "I prefer this to carrying a hard copy book or a Kindle with me. I can just put it in my pocket and don't have to carry a bag."

Caroline stuck out her lower lip and gently bobbed her head.

"I like my Kindle," she said.

Arun smiled. "What can you tell me about Katie?"

"Let's see. I am assuming you are pretty familiar with the Katie that Gabriel described to you?" Caroline paused and waited for Arun's reply.

Arun nodded.

"Okay. I can tell you about the Katie who came to work for us," Caroline said.

"Are they different?" Arun inquired.

"Are who different?"

"I mean the Katie you knew and what Gabriel describes?" Arun asked.

"Why don't you tell me after I am done?"

"Okay," replied Arun.

"Katie was a volunteer as well, just like Gabriel. She didn't work in the ICU, but in the geriatrics department. If she was in the ICU, I would have met her. Volunteers serve by helping patients to the bathroom, changing their bed sheets, and helping with random errands that come up in the department. Of course, Gabriel didn't do any of that. I am sure you can understand why, but other volunteers do. They work under the direction of nurses. We love volunteers because we are always working at 150% and volunteers help reduce our workload a bit. The bad part is that volunteers are unreliable workers. First, the quality of work you get from volunteers always varies. Some are great, but some just make our job even harder. How does working at 170% sound to you?" Caroline cupped the stone table with both palms and leaned forward.

"Not good," Arun replied, shaking his head.

Caroline leaned back and said, "Second, they are volunteers and can leave anytime without warning. So, we cannot give any meaningful work to them. Just a few things here and there. There is also HIPPA, do you know what that is?"

Arun shook his head.

Caroline described what HIPAA was and how they regulated what volunteers could and could not do in a medical setting.

"Katie was one of the good ones, I hear. I didn't work with her, like I said before. But Gabriel made her pretty famous among us nurses. Rose was happy, too, that her grandchild had finally made a friend, a good friend."

"Did Rose ever talk to Katie?" Arun asked

"I don't know for sure. One day Rose told me that Katie had left the hospital without saying anything to Gabriel and that it had devastated him. I have never seen Rose so mad in all the years I've worked with her. If you ask me, Katie was probably just being nice to this special child and spoke a few nice words. She probably didn't think too much of it when it was time to move on to bigger and better things. Gabriel, on the other hand, took Katie's 'being nice' as the greatest friendship in the world. Simple misplaced expectation if you ask me . . . Rose was blind when it came to Gabriel. You have to understand, she raised a special child with much care and love."

She looked at her watch, put her palms on the stone table, leaned forward and said, "I have to go, sorry."

"Oh, no problem. Thank you again for meeting with me in such short notice," Arun replied.

"I hope you got what you were looking for?" Caroline asked.

Arun smiled and said, "To be honest with you, I don't think I was looking for anything. I was only curious and wanted to make sure that he was seeing someone who could help him with his mental state."

"Mental state?" Caroline knitted her eyebrows, cocked her head.

"Uh-huh, his dreams and Ka—" Arun was interrupted by a beeping sound coming from Caroline's purse.

"It's my pager. I must go. I hope you get a chance to talk to Rose about your concerns. It was nice to meet you." Caroline picked up her bag and the lunch box, and hurried back the way she came in.

Arun watched Caroline walk inside the building.

FORTY-THREE

December 2016

A month later, Arun found himself sitting in the same spot waiting for Rose Galligar. Arun had never met Rose before, so he looked around to see if he could spot a woman who was also looking around. He saw none. Several people were coming out to the courtyard and going inside the cafeteria through the same door that Caroline had used last month.

"Hi," said a voice from his left.

A woman wearing a hospital uniform was standing next to him.

What do they call these uniforms?

Arun had seen nurses wearing these at the Worcester Memorial hospital as well. Maybe all nurses wore the same uniform, just like a white lab coat for all doctors. Actually, that wasn't true though, was it? The uniform styles were the same, but the colors and patterns would vary from hospital to hospital. Uniform colors that he had seen before ranged from navy blue, sky blue, red, pink, to what this woman was wearing today—

aqua green.

Scrubs . . . that's it! Scrubs . . . Was Caroline wearing scrubs too? He couldn't remember.

It was a bright, sunny day, just like the last time. This woman looked good in her aqua green scrubs. Probably in her late thirties or early forties, he thought.

"Hi," Arun replied.

"I am Rose," the woman said.

Arun leaned back in disbelief; he wasn't expecting Gabriel's grandmother to be this young. She could've qualified to be his mother.

"Hi, I am Arun Shah." They shook hands and Arun offered her a seat across from his.

Once she settled, he said, "I am sorry if I looked startled to you, I was looking for a grandmother. You did not fit the profile in my head."

Rose smiled and then threw her head back with a hearty laugh. "How nice of you to say that. Thank you! I had my daughter when I was twenty-one and she had Gabriel when she was nineteen. So, yeah, I became a grandmother when I was forty." She gave another hearty laugh. "Women these days don't have kids even in their early forties, you know? Jennifer Lopez is still not married . . . and does not have ki . . ." She paused, looked down at the stone table, screwed up her face, "I am sorry, I must be thinking about someone else, Jennifer Lopez has multiple kids I think. Oh . . . yes . . . she is so goddamn hot at this age. That's what her issue is, she is so hot. I confused her with some other celebrity whose issue was not having a baby." She threw her head back and laughed again.

Arun just smiled.

"So, Caroline tells me that you were concerned about Gabriel. She didn't know why. Is everything okay?" Her smile was gone from her face, and was now replaced by genuine concern.

Arun described everything from the start. How he'd met Gabriel, the primary focus of their discussion—Katie—his concern for Gabriel, and how that conversation helped Arun get out of his own doom and gloom mental state.

"Thank you for saying that A-roon. Did I say it correctly?"

"Yep . . ." Arun replied. There were more important things at hand than correct pronunciation of his name.

Rose smiled. Perhaps feeling proud that she'd nailed it, Arun thought. "After his mother died of postpartum infection, my husband and I raised him as our child. It is hard enough to raise a child who needs constant supervision, then there is all the self-doubt. Am I doing enough? Could I do more? What is everyone thinking? It goes on and on and on. Every now and then when someone says something nice like you just did, it makes it all worth it. Thank you." She tilted her head to her left, extended her hand across the stone table, and put her palms on top of Arun's clasped hands. Arun thought she looked pretty. She must be in her fifties now, yet what came to his mind was *fuckable.* He shifted a little in his seat, unsure if it was Rose's touch that made him shift or his lurid thought.

She kept holding his hands, which made Arun very uncomfortable. Arun could see tears welling up in her eyes. She finally removed her hands from Arun's and searched for something in her purse. She took out a tissue and dabbed the corners of her eyes. She sniffed through her left nostril and said, "Sorry . . . thank you again."

"Hey, no problem. You don't have to thank me. I am very happy I got to meet Gabriel."

Rose smiled. She said, "Your concern is regarding Gabriel's dream, correct?"

"Yes, the way he described it to me, it sounded more like a hallucination than a dream, but of course I am not an expert by any means. If he isn't already being looked at by an expert, could you consider it?"

"We took him earlier this year to a psychiatrist. Her conclusion was that it indeed seemed like a dream and medications wouldn't be effective. She said you could still dream under the influence of a strong sedative. I talked to her about hallucinations too, you know, maybe just the drug would help him? But she didn't think that would be necessary. She did ask us to monitor his sleep though. We did. He sleeps very well. I guess that is why he is dreaming. Did you know that you dream during the deepest cycle of your sleep?"

Arun shook his head.

"It's like dreams confirm that you are in a deep sleep." She smiled. "We monitored anyway. But everything was normal. She also asked us to monitor any unusual activities or behaviors, and that is why I have asked people at Worcester Hospital to inform me if they notice any anomalies. I again thank you for keeping an eye on my child." She paused and looked at Arun. When she saw that he had nothing to add, she said, "Anything else

A-roon that you noticed?"

Arun thought for a few seconds and said, "He seemed blue. But I think it was because of his latest dream. It sounded awful."

Rose nodded. "Yes, he is usually a cheerful boy. That was an awful dream. He tells me he hasn't had any more since then?" She gave a questioning look.

"Yeah, that is what he told me too," Arun replied.

"Oh . . . thank God." She sighed.

FORTY-FOUR

A run thought Rose was very warm and easy to talk to. She inquired about the doom and gloom comment he had made earlier. He explained. His happy marriage, his son, and his unfortunate affair. She listened. He talked. Arun realized that he hadn't told his story to anyone else since he'd described it to the police. It felt cathartic every time he got it off his chest.

Rose held his hand again and he felt genuine empathy. She chose her profession well, he thought. She had a beautiful face. Amazing! If you considered her age. It was almost as if she hadn't aged beyond forty. Arun had seen quite a few examples of non-aging men and women among celebrities, but among average people, she was the first one. She carried herself well. Her face was tight, bright, and she had applied just the right amount of makeup. He briefly looked below her neck. The scrubs covered what he was trying to peek at, but he could see the size and the shape.

Good, he thought. Again, amazing considering her age. He instinctively pulled back his eyes and looked at her to make sure she didn't catch his little adventure. She was looking straight at him. He couldn't tell for sure, but she was smiling, so he assumed she hadn't. All in all, what an amazing woman, Arun thought. If there was one thing that Arun didn't like about Rose, it was her ears. They were awfully small!

FORTY-FIVE

The next morning Arun woke up refreshed. He hadn't felt this way in a long time. He was at peace. Sara and her memory weren't haunting him today. He had coffee and bread with hazelnut spread for breakfast. He thought about his meeting with Rose. She had thanked him for saying that Gabriel helped him. It had meant a lot to her.

Arun hadn't thought much about why he was investigating Gabriel's life. He wasn't looking for a pat on his back, or any other form of reward. He didn't have any expectations. His only desire was to do the right thing. The right thing was to make sure Gabriel's loved ones knew what was going on. And they knew. His job was done. He finished his bread and coffee with that thought.

As he was rinsing his plate and cup, another thought popped up in his mind out of nowhere. It said the job was not done. Gabriel didn't know what had happened to his mother. He had some ideas based on Katie's hypothesis but those were only hypotheses, not proof. Arun didn't have any proof either, but now Arun knew for sure based on what Rose had told him, which was as close to proof as you could get. Gabriel should know. He wasn't going to tell Gabriel his source, no need to create friction between Gabriel and Rose. He could just tell Gabriel that he found out from the city archives or something. A little white lie would be okay. What mattered was the intention, which was to bring some closure into Gabriel's life about his mother. Arun understood what it was like not knowing what had happened to your loved ones. Sara wasn't related to him, legally or by blood, but she ranked high on his list of loved ones. Arun was reminded time and again of what was Sara's mostly likely fate. Only recently he had read in the newspaper about Kristen Cabo of Arizona.

Kristen was a dancer at a club. Twelve years ago, she had left work at 11:35 PM and hadn't been seen since. Her mother had known for a while that she might not be found alive, but she had said that knowing would bring peace to her family.

Arun knew many would say that Sara's fate would be like Kristen's, only waiting to be discovered in bones in a ravine or under a pit. But that wasn't enough. Hypotheses were never enough. One needed proof. Like Kristen's mother said, knowing would bring peace. Gabriel deserved peace, too.

So, he decided to see Gabriel one more time.

FORTY-SIX

A run went to Worcester Memorial Hospital and received a visitor's pass to the ICU. He walked over to the nurses' station and saw a new nurse behind the station desk. Not anyone he recognized from his stay. He wasn't sure if she would know Gabriel but was delighted to find out that she did. She told him Gabriel wasn't in today. Today was Friday and Gabriel didn't work on Fridays, only Wednesday and Thursday.

Arun knew that, didn't he? Well, too bad. He should have remembered that before coming over. How was Arun related to Gabriel, the nurse had asked. He briefly described how he met Gabriel, his concerns for him, and yesterday's meeting with Rose. She nodded and smiled. He thanked the new nurse, who was apparently not so new, just new to him.

Arun was about to turn around.

"Poor Gabriel," she said.

Arun stopped.

"When he was born, I wondered what would happen to him. I am happy that Rose and people like you are in his life." Saying this, she bobbed her head and looked down at a document that was lying on the desk in front of her.

"You've known Gabriel since his birth?" Arun asked.

She looked up and said, "Oh yeah . . . He was born in this hospital. I worked at the birthing center back then. Right off the bat, things were stacked against him, you know. He was born with a genetic defect, then his mother rejected him, and oh then what happened to his mother . . ."

Arun interjected, "You mean postpartum infection?"

She looked at him as if he was crazy. "No. I mean her suicide, or at least allegedly," she said.

"WHAT?"

"Yes . . . I thought you knew since you said you met Rose?"

"But Rose . . ."

"Oh . . . Rose was devastated when her only child committed suicide," she said.

Arun was still in shock but managed to ask, "But WHY?"

"Who knows. A nurse who was in the delivery room that day claimed that the new mother had refused skin to skin and breastfeeding . . . she apparently screamed to get the baby out of her sight . . . 'abomination' the new mother had allegedly cried. There was a lot of screaming in that birthing room. Rose was irate, and after they took baby Gabriel to the neonatal unit, mother and daughter started a screaming match. Rose's daughter apparently kept saying, 'you could have stopped this. You could have stopped this' . . . something like that. Two days later, we found her daughter hung from the ceiling fan . . ."

Arun looked at the nurse, his mouth agape. He swallowed and mumbled, "That is awful!"

He looked at the floor, unable to decide what to make of this, or whether to make anything of it. His musings were interrupted by the sound of something touching the desktop. He looked up and saw that the nurse had placed her reading glasses on the desk and was studying him. Her body had slouched, and she sighed before saying, "Look, you seem like a nice man, I should not say this, but I know I won't be able to sleep well if I don't say this to you. You befriending Gabriel is very sweet and all, but I have to warn you."

Arun knitted his eyebrows.

The nurse looked around. Finding nobody paying attention to their conversation, she stepped outside the nurses' station and walked over to a corner with a few chairs and soda machines. Arun followed her with his eyes but he didn't move. She stopped near a soda machine, turned around, folded her arms and looked at Arun.

Arun reluctantly walked over to the nurse and stood a couple of feet away from her.

She closed her eyes, took a deep breath, and said, "Can you promise me what I am going to say next will be just between you and me?"

FORTY-SEVEN

The nurse talked; Arun listened. After talking for more than ten minutes, she sighed and said, "What I just told you, I haven't even told my husband . . . But I felt like this was your business to know, to know what you are getting yourself into."

Arun was still in shock, trying to digest everything the nurse had shared, when he heard his name called from behind.

"Arun. Mr. Shah, is that you?"

Arun turned around and saw Ann Horowitz, one of the nurses who had taken care of him when he was admitted to the hospital.

Arun waved his hand at Ann before turning back to see the other nurse, but she was already walking back to the nurses' station. Arun walked over to Ann and offered his hand.

Ann ignored his offer and threw her arms around him and hugged him.

"How have you been, Arun? What's wrong? You look like you just saw a ghost." Ann's bright eyes were staring at Arun, her hands grabbing his arms.

He pulled himself together and said in a low tone, "Just been a long day I . . . I am doing well, Ann."

"Gabriel is magic, isn't he? I have no idea how he does this," Ann replied.

Arun managed to smile and told her he was there to see him. He forgot Gabriel only worked on Wednesdays and Thursdays. He would come back next week.

"I don't know if that would be necessary, Arun." Ann looked solemn.

"What do you mean?" Arun asked.

"His grandmother called yesterday and said that Gabriel wouldn't be coming in going forward. Something to do with his health, she said."

"WHAAAT?" Arun gave an incredulous look to Ann.

Ann shrugged. "Yeah, I know . . . We liked to have him around, too. He had an uplifting energy. Too bad. We cannot force his grandmother. Besides, if it is his health, we shouldn't force it. Hopefully, he will feel better soon and maybe he will be able to come in again."

"Did she say what health issue?" Arun asked.

Ann shook her head.

"I . . ." Arun thought about talking to Ann about his meeting with Gabriel's grandmother and what the nurse at the nurses' station had just told him. But he stopped himself.

He just shook his head in disbelief.

"I know," Ann said and shrugged again.

"Do you have a contact number for Gabriel?" Arun asked.

"His grandmother was our usual contact," Ann replied.

Arun was still shaking his head. He couldn't believe what he had just heard. Rose didn't mention anything when they met yesterday.

Could the nurse be right?

"Folks in volunteer services may have additional contact information. They are the ones who assign volunteers to different departments," Ann said.

"Arun! . . . Arun!!" Ann snapped her fingers in front of Arun's face.

"Wake up, man!" Ann laughed.

Arun gently shook his head and said, "When did she call you?"

"Yesterday, like I said," Ann replied.

"Did you talk to her?"

"I actually did, I was at the desk when she called to let us know."

"Do you remember the time?"

"Mm . . . let me think . . . I came back from my smoking break . . . sometime in the afternoon. I don't know the exact time."

"Do you have a timestamp logged in your computer for when you took the break?"

"We don't flip burgers, Mr. Shah. We don't have a timesheet." Ann looked annoyed.

Arun held his arms up. "Sorry, didn't mean it that way. I don't know. I don't know. Sorry, Ann."

"That's ok. Why do you need to know the specific time anyway?"

This time he told her. But only about the meeting with Rose and how she had lied about the cause of her daughter's death. "Can you think a little harder?" Arun pleaded.

"Well, I went to room 105, took a smoke break, and came back. Rose's call came just a little after. Let's see . . . um . . ." Ann raised her brows and her eyes brightened. "I gave Mr. Stevenson in 105 his medication and I should have noted the time for that."

"That sounds promising!" Arun agreed.

"Ok. Let me find out," Ann said. She was gone for less than five minutes, but for Arun it felt like an hour.

"So, 1:15 was room 105. 15-minute smoke break, plus 5 minutes to walk back. Another 5 to 10 minutes after that, I was back at the nurses' station . . ." Ann started to count with her fingers and announced, "1:45 PM . . . somewhere around there would be my guess."

Arun did his own finger counting and concluded that was when his meeting with Rose had ended. Now that he thought about it, Rose had stood up from the stone bench and headed back the way she came. When she had opened the door to the building, she held the door handle with her left hand and held a black object on her right ear.

Cell phone?

He looked up at Ann. She had a questioning look. He raised his eyebrows and said, "Thank you so much for finding this for me. I have to go . . ." Ann's expression tried to protest but Arun read it before she could articulate. "I can't explain. Please. Thank you. I have to go now." He turned around and went toward the elevator.

Ann stood motionless with folded hands and knitted brows.

FORTY-EIGHT

July 31st, 2016

C huck Lagano walked out of the store. He was surprised at what had just happened. This very attractive sales associate had agreed to ride with him in his car.

Fucking awesome.

He hurried to his car. She could come out any minute. He needed to be prepared. He opened the door to the driver's side and sat behind the wheel.

Think. Think. Think.

He looked to his right. On the passenger seat was a bag with prescription medication he had picked up that morning from CVS before coming to Greenmile Walk. He smiled. He grabbed a Pepsi bottle from the cup holder. He opened the cap of the medicine bottle and took out one pill. He looked around. He closed the Pepsi bottle, placed the pill on the elbow rest, and smacked it with the back of the Pepsi bottle. He repeated this a few times until the pill turned into powder. Chuck was unsure how many he would need to make her pass out. He only took one at night, and only occasionally. He always went to bed immediately afterward, so he didn't know how drowsy it made him.

He crushed another pill, then another, then another. Each time after he crushed, he put it in the Pepsi bottle. Was four enough? He didn't know. This thing would need to act fast on her, too. She would want to go home and she had mentioned that her boyfriend was at home too. This had to act fast. Within ten minutes maybe. He crushed three more pills and put the powder inside the Pepsi bottle. That should be enough.

He closed the Pepsi bottle and put it back in the cup holder. He closed the medicine bottle and tossed it back. He sat on his seat, satisfied. He thought about the sales girl again. He thought about undressing her. She would be sleeping nicely after taking all those pills. He would lay on the bed and undress her.

Chuck slipped his left hand inside his trousers. She would be naked and asleep. He would kiss her body. She would taste so good. Her legs would be limp, but she would taste so good. He would spread her legs and fuck her. She would be clean shaved. Yes, Chuck would like that. Then he would fuck her. She would crease her forehead in pain. Would she remember any of this later? It didn't matter, he would fuck her. Fuck her more. Chuck lowered his trouser, pulled out his dick, and came. Chuck felt content. The sales girl would be there any minute. He reached for a tissue in the back seat and cleaned up his mess. Finally, someone to fuck. Someone so beautiful and sexy. He reached out to the back seat and grabbed a shopping bag. He took out a bikini bottom and sniffed.

FORTY-NINE

December 2016

After Jim hung up the phone, Sandra asked who it was. Jim said, "Who do you think?" There were only two people who irritated Jim. One was his mother-in-law and the other was Arun Shah. Based on the conversation Sandra had heard, she didn't think it was Karla.

"New lead on Sara, I presume?" She smiled.

"Worse. He's found a new case to entertain himself with. Some blind child who has been abused, he claims." Jim shook his head, his face visibly red. Sandra waited a few moments then cautiously added, "We shouldn't ignore it, though."

"I know we shouldn't, Sandy," Jim fumed. "If it was any other human being, I would listen but that goddamn guy just pisses me off. He needs to see a therapist, you know?"

Sandra nodded.

Jim softened his tone a little and said, "I told him to contact child services. They are the right department for these matters anyway. Let them deal with him. Who knows? He may find some other Jim to pester. God! I hope."

Sandra gave a crooked smile.

Her phone vibrated. She pulled out her phone from the back pocket and looked at the screen. It read, "Do not tell Jim, please!"

"What is it?" Jim inquired.

She froze.

Sandra sat in silence, staring at the screen.

"Sandy? You ok?" Jim came closer.

She put the phone on silent and back in her pocket. She said, "Just a friend. I will text her back later."

"Friend? Since when, Sandy?" Jim asked. This brought a smile on his face.

Sandra smiled too.

She had gone home early that afternoon. About 4 PM, she remembered that weird text message from Mr. None-Other-Than. She got up from her couch and went over to the dining table where she had left her phone. She looked at her messages app and the number "5" flashed in red. She pressed the app. All five messages were under one name.

Arun Shah (5)
Do not tell Jim, Please!   *1.45 p.m.*

(345) 992-09   *Thursday*
Sandra, your friend Melissa Tollid . . .

She pressed Arun Shah (5).

Do not tell Jim, Please!
35 Elm Street, East Hampton, CT 06044
A kid named Gabriel has been abused.

Could you check please!
Jim thinks I am a lunatic :(

The last message brought her crooked smile back. *Yes, he does.*

But she did not know how she felt about Arun. He was disturbed all right, but not irrational. He had made a very logical deduction about the stopped car. She had to convince Jim that the theory had merit and they should at least follow-up. Jim had begrudgingly agreed. But when the theory fell flat on its head, Jim was done listening to anything that came out of Arun Shah's mouth.

FIFTY

As she sat in her dining chair, drinking her evening tea, Sandra thought about the stopped car. After their meeting with the owner of the stopped car, Jim had been pissed. His anger was not directed at the woman whom they had just interviewed but at Arun. His dislike had blinded him because for the most part, Arun had been correct. There was a stopped car. There was also a traffic pattern at Greenmile walk between 3:40 PM and 3:45 PM on July 31st. The story only differed regarding what happened after the car stopped. Arun claimed, without evidence, that Sara must have climbed inside the stopped car. "Could you please check on that?" Arun had requested. He'd made that request almost every week with some new theory. Jim received most of these requests and was getting beyond tired. He was mad. Disgust consumed his expression when he heard Arun's name.

On the other hand, the woman . . .

what was her name again?

. . . had explained that the car was stopped because she and her husband were fighting, and they left after a few minutes. This woman didn't even know that Jim and Sandra were inquiring about a stopped car, but she described everything in great detail. Her story checked out with everything they had observed on the CCTV footage. Of course, there were parts of her story that weren't available on CCTV footage, and for those parts, it was Arun's hypothesis versus her description. Or as Jim liked to say *her detailed logical explanation versus a lunatic's hypothesis.* "It's a no brainer, Sandy!" Jim had told her.

Sandra couldn't disagree, but she couldn't jump on a "no brainer" train either. Something about that woman bugged her. A voice deep inside of her, where logic did not work, where analytics did not mean much, felt uneasy. Sandra did not ignore this voice. She had followed up on her intuition and checked out license plates for more cars that would've had to have passed the stopped car on July 31st. To her surprise, many drivers remembered that day well. They gave her the same reason that the woman from the stopped car had given—they realized they were at the same place where Sara was last seen.

Many drivers also remembered the stopped car that had annoyed them very much. But nothing else—not the color of the car, the make and model, not even what side of the road it was parked on. Sandra got only inconsistent answers. Did they see who was in the car? Or how many people? Again, no consistent answer. There was one guy who had said that the driver was a male who wore a hat and they flipped the bird at each other; he did not see anyone else in the stopped car. But there were other drivers who had claimed there were five passengers, no it was a truck not a sedan, yes, a woman driver . . . nothing there to convince the D.A. to approve a search warrant. Her gut was still unhappy, but she couldn't do anything else . . . *What was that woman's name again?*

FIFTY-ONE

Arun opened his eyes. He was looking up at a white ceiling. He blinked. His head ached; it felt like it was going to crack open. He tried to move his mouth, but it wouldn't open. He couldn't talk. The pain had now shifted to his mouth. It was burning. He couldn't tell what was happening, but his mouth wouldn't open. The more he tried to open it, the more it ached. The pain shifted to his wrist. He tried to look at his wrist, but he couldn't. He couldn't lift his head. Was he paralyzed? Was he dreaming? What was happening? Where was he? He moved his whole body, his head, legs, wrists. He screamed. His mouth didn't open but he could hear his throaty cry. He also heard the sound of metal clanking as he moved his hands and feet. He slowly understood. No, he wasn't paralyzed. No, he wasn't dreaming. He was chained to a bed—by the sound of it, a metal bed.

His mouth would still not open and it burned like hell. His head was strapped to the bed. He could only move his eyeballs. In his field of vision, he only saw the white ceiling. He panicked. He kept moving his hands and legs violently, but he couldn't do it for more than a few minutes at a time. He soon saw the futility of it. He was tired; he dozed off.

A door opened to his left and he woke up. He strained his eye socket to see to his left, but he saw nothing. The door closed. He heard a lock, a click, then another, then another, then another.

A woman.

He stared at her face. She looked at him and smiled, towering over his face. He blinked his eyes to see if he could get a clearer image, perhaps a different image. But no.

Rose?

FIFTY-TWO

Earlier at the Worcester
Memorial Hospital

The nurse looked around. She saw that nobody was paying attention to their conversation, so she stepped outside the nurses' station and walked over to a corner with a few chairs and soda machines. Arun followed her with his eyes but he didn't move. She stopped near a soda machine, turned around, folded her arms and looked at Arun.

Arun reluctantly walked over to the nurse and stood a couple of feet away from her. She grabbed his right arm and said in a hushed voice, "If I were you, I would be very careful befriending Gabriel."

"Why?" Arun asked.

The nurse sighed. "Rose is very weird about Gabriel . . ." She thought for a few seconds and continued, "Perhaps weird is not the right word . . . I cannot quite describe it . . ." She sighed again.

Arun saw desperation in her eyes; she wanted him to understand, he could tell, but he could also see her disappointment because he wasn't getting it.

She closed her eyes, took a deep breath, and said, "Can you promise me that what I am going to say next will be just between you and me?"

Arun nodded. "Sure."

"I could lose my job over this so please . . . I am only saying this because I am concerned about you."

"You can trust me . . . Ms . . ."

"My name is not important . . . it is better actually if you don't know my name because I will deny every single word if this ever comes out . . . but I am really hoping that it does not . . ."

"Please feel free," Arun said and placed his left hand on her right arm. It looked like they were going to embrace each other.

Arun pulled his hands back; the nurse did the same. She clasped her hands and brought them in front of her chest and said, "This was ten years ago, some kid was giving Gabriel a hard time at school. Name calling, pushing, shoving, that kind of stuff . . ."

Arun nodded.

"After a while, Gabriel didn't want to go to school. Rose didn't know what had happened and Gabriel wouldn't say anything. Unbeknownst to Gabriel, she fit a nanny cam or spy cam or something like that in his backpack and sent him to school. A couple of days later this bully kid went home with his left eye all swollen up. He kept telling his parents that he needed to repent because of how he had treated Gabriel. His parents accused Gabriel of assault. But of course, no one believed Gabriel could do something like that. Besides, everyone had seen Gabriel at the Special Olympics tryouts at the gym that afternoon when the assault had allegedly happened.

The school launched a brief investigation but nothing came out of it. The principal herself had seen Gabriel the entire afternoon, so he couldn't have beaten the bully kid, the principal concluded. Anyway, a few months later the bully kid's parents pulled him out of the school. He had developed mental health problems. He had been a normal kid before the incident, a bully but normal otherwise, but afterwards he became depressed and self-destructive. He needed to punish himself, he would say. Doctors couldn't figure it out either. His mother lamented that it was as if someone had rewired his brain for self-destruction. Of course, she meant metaphorically, but I think that is literally what happened."

"You think . . ."

The nurse continued, "Yes, I think this was all Rose. I don't know how she did this, especially the rewiring stuff. And I don't want to know either. But the moral of this story is clear to me—keep a healthy distance from Gabriel. I do. Like I said, Rose is weird about him."

She frowned and seemed to say to herself, "I still cannot think of the right word, it is more than just weird."

"But unlike the bully kid, I genuinely want to help Gabriel not hurt him," Arun said hopefully.

"I know you do. I am just saying that you need to be careful . . . I had to say this to you, the rest is up to you . . ." Saying this, the nurse stared over Arun's head. She looked pensive.

Arun raised his arm to bring her back from her trance.

"Sorry," she said. "It's just that I have wondered about her daughter as well . . ."

"Her suicide?" Arun asked.

"and Gary."

"Who's Gary?"

The nurse shook her head as if to get rid of her current train of thoughts and said, "It's nothing . . . old mind thinks crazy things . . . do you know about Katie?" she asked.

Arun nodded.

"Of course, everyone who knows Gabriel knows Katie," the nurse said.

They both smiled and nodded their head in unison.

"After Katie left and after I saw the fury in Rose's eyes, I wondered what would happen to Katie, you know. Rose was mad with the bully kid, but with Katie, she was vein-popping furious."

She laughed. "I even checked Google to see if there was anything on the news about Katie becoming mentally sick and self-destructive, like the bully kid. But of course, there was nothing like that on the news"

Arun didn't say anything.

The nurse said, "Maybe you are right. Maybe Katie and you are different cases. Both of you love Gabriel and Gabriel loves you. It is different than the bully kid who was intentionally harming him. Besides, you are a grown man. Take what I said for what it's worth. But do not ever bring this up with Rose or anyone else. Please!"

"I won't, trust me," Arun said.

"Take care." The nurse smiled, touched Arun's arm again, and walked back toward the nurses' station.

"Um . . . Ms . . ." Arun said.

The nurse stopped and turned around.

Arun walked closer to her and said, "How do you know all of this?"

The nurse smiled. "Well, we live in the same town, East Hampton. I have also worked with Rose for more than twenty years. I am probably the only one in this whole wide world whom she thinks as her friend. And I am. Like any good friend, I know her luminous side as well as her dark side. Most of the people who know her only see the nice friendly person, soft spoken, deeply caring. And she can be nice, don't get me wrong. But if you get on her wrong side, she will still appear to you as the nicest person in the world, except something ominous will be brewing inside of her. When that happens . . . good luck! I fear her dark side."

She sighed and continued, "What I just told you, I haven't even told my husband. Mostly because it is none of his business and the moment I tell him, he will want me to unfriend Rose. You see, once you befriend someone like Rose, you cannot undo that. All you can do is maintain a healthy distance. My husband will not understand this and so it's not worth bringing it up to him. But I felt like this was your business to know, to know what you are getting yourself into."

FIFTY-THREE

Arun wondered what he really had gotten himself into. He rubbed his eyes again. It was Rose. He violently moved his hands and legs again and screamed. Screamed with all his might. His face turned purple and the veins on his neck bulged. She stepped back a little, not holding on to the bed railings anymore. The bed was moving violently. Arun was upset.

She threw her head back and laughed. Her laughter matched Arun's throaty cry and the sound of chains clanking against the bed. The laughter stopped. Arun stopped. Next, he heard a mechanical sound coming from under the bed and slowly his bed rose up. He could now see his bare legs chained to the other end of the metal bed. He could see more.

He was wearing black underwear, but shiny . . . no . . . was that leather underwear? The rest of his body was bare. Rose was still standing to his left. She was grinning. She moved her hand to the back of her head and untied her ponytail. She shook her head, and her red hair flew down to her shoulders. She grinned again. The same person who'd looked like an angel last time they met now looked terrifying. Arun saw something else too. A guy was sitting on another metal bed, which was few steps behind where Rose was standing. He was wearing a camo hat, a white T-shirt, blue jeans, and . . . Arun couldn't see below his waist. The guy wasn't looking at Arun; he was looking at something next to him, on the bed, behind Rose.

Arun looked at Rose; she was staring right back at him. That reminded him of his earlier encounter with Rose. She never looked away, did she? Now he knew for sure that she had caught him. She had caught him taking a peek at her chest. *Is that what this is all about?*

Rose was still smiling at him; her red hair looked like fire above her head. Arun was now looking at her eyes, and she was staring at his. She looked down below her neck, and Arun followed her gaze. She looked back at him. He met her gaze. She laughed. It was no longer a hearty laugh.

"You thought I didn't notice, A-roon?" she asked.

"I notice everything." She laughed again.

"You wanted to find out what's down here, didn't you?" Rose bit her lower lips and looked down below her neck again.

Rose squeezed the sides of her breasts and bent down, revealing her cleavage. She took out her blood red tongue and licked her lips in a slow circling motion.

She took her top off. She took two steps closer to Arun's bed and cupped Arun's underwear with her left hand, slowly squeezing what she grabbed. When Rose came closer to the bed, Arun could now see what was behind her, what the man was looking at. Arun turned pale.

Rose kept massaging his dick gently. She caressed and kissed his inner thighs. She threw herself on top of Arun and sat on his dick. She was only in her red bra and red panties. She rubbed her panties against his underwear. She looked at him. His face was pale, and his eyes were wide open. He wasn't even looking at her. His head was turned to his left and he was staring at the girl who was sitting on the other bed, next to the man. The girl was naked just like Arun. Bare on top and bottom, wearing only black leather underwear. Unlike him though, she was sitting on the bed, looking down in front of her. Only her right hand was tied to the bed frame.

"Snap out of it!" Rose said, snapping her fingers.

Arun was startled and looked at Rose. He wanted to say something, but he couldn't. His eyes, however, looked like they would pop out of his sockets.

"Shhhh." Rose put her right index finger over her lips, which were decorated with the brightest red hue. "Look here, Mr," she said and put her index finger in her mouth and started sucking. She cupped her right breast with her left hand and kneaded. Arun's eyes rolled back to the left side of his bed. Rose sighed, looked down, and checked Arun's limp dick.

Fuck.

She jumped on the floor and took two steps closer to where Arun's head was. Once Arun could no longer ignore her,

SLAP!

SLAP!

"Easy, Rose, you don't want to knock him out again," the man behind Rose spoke for the first time.

"Shut up, Gary! You got it fucking easy. Turn the whore whichever fucking way you want and fuck her. Fuck, fuck, fuck, until you fucking want. Toss her on the bed when you are done . . . I have to get this motherfucker excited first," Rose shot back.

"You were doing good. Even I got a boner watching you do your old tricks! Look!" Gary grabbed his dick from outside his jeans. He was grinning, showing four teeth and otherwise mostly empty space inside his mouth.

Rose smiled. "Awww . . . you old fuck! That's why I love you. Always ready like a horse. But stop showing those non-existent teeth. I told you to put those dentures on before coming to this room . . . yuck!" Rose quivered.

Gary took out a plastic box from his jeans' back pocket, took out his dentures, and put them inside his mouth. He shot a Colgate smile back at Rose. "Ah! That is much better," Rose said, ruffling his hair. "Now if I could only get this motherfucker to fuck me . . . I would call it a day. I have an early morning shift at the hospital." Rose said.

"Why don't you let her try?" Gary raised his chin and pointed to the girl sitting next to him on the bed. Rose looked at her.

"If he was staring at her . . ." Gary leaned closer to Rose's ear and whispered, "maybe he was looking for a young pussy." He leaned back and laughed hysterically. He almost fell off the bed railing.

Rose shot him a look that seemed to say, *Soon you will be tied to the bed as well.* He raised his hands up and said, "No harm in trying. If she can get it hard, you can jump on it. When inside a wet pussy, it will stay hard, baby, biology will take over. Not'ing he can do about it."

Rose stared at Gary. She looked at the girl with disgust, then looked back at Gary. "How are you going to put her on top of that bed?" she said, pointing to the bed Arun was tied in.

"Untie her from this bed, put her on the other bed," Gary replied matter of factly.

Rose raised her brows, her eyes widened. "Untie? Are you crazy, old man. We have never untied her."

Suddenly Arun was out of a trance. He had heard the conversation between Rose and Gary, but his brain wasn't reacting to anything. His brain had frozen, and all he could do was stare at the girl sitting next to the man. Now he was out of this comatose state and he felt sadness. He wasn't thinking of himself; he was sad for the girl. She was still looking down at the floor. She hadn't shown any reaction to anything. She hadn't even turned her head. She had a single cuff on her right wrist. Her legs dangled down from the edge of the bed. She looked less like a human and more like a badly kept manikin.

"*Orange, yellow, and brown dress and black hems. She is always looking away, maybe on the floor or towards the other wall. I can tell because I see only a black hue where her head should be . . .*" *Gabriel had said.*

KATIE!!! Arun screamed inside his head. But that didn't stop his face from turning red and his eyes widening in horror.

What kind of psychos are these two?

Arun's thoughts were broken by the clank of metal. His eyes followed the source of the sound and saw that Gary was opening Katie's cuffs. Rose was standing in front of them pointing a gun at Katie. What had he missed? He had zoned out, ruminating on his predicament. But he noticed that there was no tension in their demeanor. Rose and Gary were calm, and Katie continued to have no reaction.

Rose stepped forward and grabbed Katie's jaw and raised it with her left hand. "If you do anything stupid, anything, remember that I am not going to kill you. I am going to kill that guy and leave him in this room. You will live with a dead body for weeks, smelling it as it rots. I am not going to give you anything to eat either. So, when you are beyond hungry, you can eat the decaying remains of a dead man. You got it?"

Rose was talking about killing Arun, but instead of feeling fear,

Arun felt anger. Katie, on the other hand, did not say anything. She continued to not react. Rose removed her left hand from Katie's jaw. Katie's head slumped like a dead woman's and then *SLAP!* Rose held Katie's jaw again and pressed her cheeks, *SLAP!*

"Don't you ignore me cunt."

SLAP!

SLAP!

"YOU HEAR ME?" Rose screamed at the top of her lungs.

Arun wondered, how come Gabriel did not hear all this? Or did he hear and just stayed in his room, scared and unable to move? Rose had probably given similar threats to the poor kid. How come he hadn't said any of this to Arun?

Then Arun noticed something that he hadn't noticed before. The room was brightly lit. Was it night already? He couldn't tell. It was late in the afternoon when he'd come to check on Gabriel but there was still some daylight left. He had knocked on the door and Rose had opened it. She was very happy to see him and took him to the kitchen. She'd made them coffee and asked him for the reason for his visit. Arun hadn't planned this very well. He was worried about Gabriel but what was he planning to say to Rose?

That he thought he couldn't trust Rose anymore?

That he didn't understand why she had called the hospital to pull out Gabriel right after their meeting?

That he didn't understand why she had lied about her daughter's suicide?

None of these proved she was abusing Gabriel, but Arun felt something sinister. Those couldn't be coincidences, he thought. He was getting too close to her grandchild and she was worried Arun would find something unpleasant. Yes, that made sense to him. But what was she afraid of? What was she hiding?

That was what he'd wanted to ask her. That was why he had come over to her house. But he couldn't say any of this. He had told her he just wanted to see Gabriel. Rose first smiled, then laughed. Her usual booming laughter. She had told him Gabriel was taking a nap in the other room and she would go check. She came back and told him Gabriel was still sleeping but he should wake up anytime now. She was standing next to Arun, to his left. Arun was sitting on a chair, looking up at her. She smiled, he smiled back. He suddenly felt a prick on the right side of his neck. Arun put his hand over his neck. Rose quickly apologized; it was her nail, she had said. They talked for a few more minutes and then the room had started spinning. He was about to fall backward when Rose grabbed his hand. She pulled him toward her and put his head on the dining table. The last thing Arun had heard was Rose instructing him to go to sleep.

Arun snapped back to present. Rose had a murderous look in her eyes and was holding Katie by her hair. Katie looked up and said, "Yes, I understand."

FIFTY-FOUR

Y es, I understand," Katie said again.

Her voice was surprisingly calm, and without any emotion. Arun still couldn't see her face but there was something familiar about her voice.

Sara? Arun thought. This wasn't the first time he had likened Sara's voice to a stranger's. After Sara disappeared, he had turned around many times thinking he had heard Sara's voice. But when Katie stood up and looked at Arun, his face turned pale as if he had seen a ghost.

Arun blinked his eyes and looked at her again. *Sara.* He squeezed his eyes harder. *Sara.* Again. *Sara.* He panicked and started to rattle the bed. He moved his limbs with fury. Closed his eyes and started screaming. His muffled scream was the loudest they had heard today. His neck veins were almost popping out. Tears rolled down his cheeks.

The naked woman curiously looked at this pathetic man. She couldn't say who had been dealt a worse hand. He had just arrived today. She had been in that room for a long time. How long, she couldn't tell. There were no clocks or calendar and she was chained all the time. But at least she was free right now. The poor guy was chained from head to toe; he couldn't even move his head and they had . . . what was that? His mouth was stained with blood and . . . was that a stitch?

OH GOD!

She looked at Rose in disbelief. Rose was smiling, looking at this man. Gary turned around and met her eyes. "Go on now, do what you do for me sweetie," ordered the old fuck.

She looked at this man, who was still moving violently with all he had. Gary wanted her to climb on the bed and start sucking this man's dick. But if she climbed on this bed, this guy would knock her out for good. She was looking at Gary, who was grinning and signaling her to *go on*, when she noticed something on this man's right inner thigh. A brown spot about three inches long and an inch wide. How odd, she thought. She knew at least one other person who had a similar birthmark in the same spot. She looked at his face again. It was beyond recognizable. His head was strapped to the bed, like in a mental hospital before electroshock therapy; his mouth was stitched and bloodied, and he had closed his eyes. She looked at the birthmark again. She looked at his whole body again. His face again.

Tears started rolling down her cheeks.

"Oh great!" cried Gary. "Fucking crying contest now." Gary threw his hands up, which immediately came down crashing on his thighs. "Good luck getting your boy toy up and running now," he said to Rose.

Arun stopped his fury. He slowly opened his eyes and looked at the girl who looked like Sara. She matched his gaze. Arun could confirm what Gary was describing. Tears were rolling down her cheeks. No, it wasn't one of the Sara lookalikes he had imagined many times for the past few months. This time, this was Sara for real. She was standing in front of him. She had recognized him. *I found you, Sara,* he wanted to say. *Alive . . . I found you alive . . .* at least physically alive. What they had done to her, what she must have been through . . . His anger was back. He was mad. He screamed again with all his might. He shook his limbs with fury. The metal rattled and rattled.

WHY?

He felt a soft touch on his left ankle. He slowed down. He opened his eyes. Sara was wiping her tears with her left hand and caressing his ankle with her right hand. He stopped. Sara moved her right hand from his ankle to his knees and then to his thigh. She put her other hand on the bed and climbed up on the bed. She pulled down his leather underwear. She held his penis with her left hand and licked it. Electricity rushed through Arun's body. She put it in her mouth and rocked it up and down. Arun just looked at Sara. Tears were back in his eyes. She took his penis out of her mouth. Looked up at him with wet eyes. He thought he heard a sorry. *But why?*

Then he saw why. He was hard. Rose pushed Sara out of the bed; Gary jumped quickly to catch her as well as the gun Rose had flung in the air. Rose jumped on the bed with Arun. She threw her red panties and squatted. She put three fingers in her mouth, took them out, and rubbed her pussy. She grabbed Arun's dick and put it in. She groaned. She bounced up and down. She groaned. She bounced faster. She groaned louder. She bounced more. She groaned louder . . .

She SCREAMED!

FIFTY-FIVE

The only sound in the room was of Rose's heavy breathing as she lay slumped down next to Arun's feet.

"That was a quickie, huh!!" Gary threw his head back and laughed.

Rose didn't say anything. She slowly got up. Gary was still laughing his ass off. "Fuck you, old fuck!" Rose shot back. "It had been a while since I had a young hard dick." She smiled. Gary was not laughing anymore. It was Rose's turn to laugh. And she did. Her laughter shook the whole room.

"Now that I know what gets him excited . . ." She shot a disgusted look at Sara, and then turned to Gary, "We will have plenty of longer sessions in future."

Gary rolled his eyes.

Rose outstretched her hand and looked at Gary. He understood and put the gun on her hand. At the exact moment the gun touched her palm, they heard a knock on the front door. The gun almost fell on the floor, but Rose was quick to catch it. "Who the fuck is that?" Rose looked at Gary.

"I don't know. Mail guy?" Gary replied.

Rose looked at her watch, it was 6 PM. A little late for mail delivery, she thought. She looked around the room, Gary was the only one with clothes on. But that wouldn't be helpful. The old fuck was good for nothing. She had to do everything in this house.

Rose placed the gun back on Gary's hand and said, "Listen now, Gary," her voice somber. "I have to go outside and check to see who the fuck it is. You have to control the situation here."

Gary nodded.

Rose turned to see Sara and Arun. "They seem to have some kind of love fest going on. I don't have time to explore what it is, but I will do that when I come back. But I can bet that they won't like the idea of either of them dying."

She smirked, grabbed a pillow, and tossed it toward Gary. "You put this on his head . . ." she pointed to Arun, "and point the gun at the pillow. If this bitch tries to make any sound, or this asshole starts to flutter like a fish again, or make that disgusting throaty noise, shoot him."

Gary nodded again.

"Now cuff her to that bed." She pointed to the bed Arun was tied in.

Gary followed her instructions and tied Sara's right hand to the bed railing. He looked around the floor, grabbed another cuff that was lying next to Sara's bed. He cuffed her left hand to Arun's bed railing as well.

"Good idea." Rose sounded pleased. She left the room immediately and closed the door behind her. Her room was across the hallway. She opened the door to her bedroom, hurried to the master bath, and jumped in the shower. She was in the shower for ten seconds, made sure her hair and the rest of her body was wet. She wrapped herself in a white bathroom gown and wrapped a towel over her head. She went out and answered the door.

FIFTY-SIX

November 2016

A fter Arun left the police station, Sandra and Jim had looked at the CCTV footage again. Arun's theory seemed to hold up. At minimum, they could not find a hole in the theory yet. The first order of business was to identify the vehicle that presumably caused the others behind it to pass from the opposite lane. The second order of business was to identify the owner of this vehicle. Jim had very reluctantly accepted that this non-cop nobody had come into their house, interfered with an on-going investigation, and punched them metaphorically with a gut-wrenching theory. What made it even more difficult to swallow was that it was a plausible theory. He admitted, this was their best lead in months. Jim was annoyed.

But after Arun left the building, the task at hand seemed simple enough. Identify the first car that was completely inside the yellow lane divider, which they did relatively quickly. Then they sent the picture of the car to the lab to get a better read on the license plate. Once a better picture came out of the lab, they ran the license plate on their system. The vehicle was registered to a man. Jim and Sandra wrote down the address on a piece of paper and headed out to meet the owner. It was only 3 PM but already getting very dark. Dark clouds loomed ominously over their heads. It would rain soon. Jim drove his black Honda Civic and Sandra sat on the front passenger seat. The street where the owner lived had rows of single family homes on both sides of the road. The road itself was very quiet. Jim's Honda Civic was the only one in motion; all of the others were parked on the side of the road.

From the opposite direction, a black pickup truck climbed up the hill and came into view. Half a minute later, Jim noticed that it was a Ford 150. But he couldn't see the driver, the window was rolled up and tinted. A mechanical voice from Jim's phone said that the destination would be 0.4 miles on the right.

Jim and Sandra climbed out of the car. Jim checked to see if the house number he had on the vehicle registration matched the house in front of them. It did. They climbed two steps to the front porch. Sandra looked for a doorbell but after not finding one, opened the door screen and knocked. A quick *tap, tap, tap.*

A woman opened the door. "Can I help you?" she said with a frown and concerned eyes.

"I am Detective Sandra Moynihan, and this is my partner, Detective Jim Kelly. Do you have a minute to talk to us about a case we are investigating?"

"Of course," she said and opened the door without hesitation. Her frown had now changed into a big smile, showing clear white teeth. Her expression was friendly and at ease.

Later Sandra would ask Jim if he thought it was odd that two police officers showed up at her door and she did not have a single concern on her face.

As they walked over to the living room, Jim asked "Is this your house?"

"Yes," the woman said, offering her hands to Jim and then to Sandra.

Jim and Sandra sat on a brown loveseat with a protective cover. The woman sat on the recliner, across from the loveseat.

"We came here looking for the owner of the car that is parked outside. Who would that be?" Jim asked.

"That would be my husband," the woman replied. "He just left a few minutes before you guys knocked on the door," she said with a smile.

"Okay. We have some questions for you regarding the disappearance of Sara Sardana. Have you heard about this case?" Jim asked.

"Of course, who hasn't in Connecticut? Besides, you must have noticed how close our house is from Greenmile Walk shopping center. As a matter of fact, we were in the shopping center when she vanished . . . or rather was kidnapped, wasn't it?"

Jim shifted a little on the loveseat and said, "We don't know what happened yet, and yes, we actually wanted to talk to you because we found out you were in the shopping center that day."

"How did you find out?" the woman asked.

"We checked the license plate number of the cars that were seen in the shopping center that day. Your car, or rather your husband's car, was one of them. We wanted to follow-up and see if you could tell us anything that could help with the investigation."

"I see. It was some time ago, but I remember a lot from that day. I don't normally remember my days this well, Mr. Kelly . . . Officer Kelly, but this day was very special. A couple of days after we went shopping, we learned about this missing girl. We soon realized that we were there. My husband and I have been watching the news about this case very religiously. It has quieted down a little now, hasn't it? I don't see it much in the news lately. Honestly, I miss it sometimes. Have you guys found something new? What do they call it . . . err . . . yeah . . . new break?" The woman looked at Jim and Sandra with a big smile. Her eyes gleamed with anticipation. It was as if she expected Jim and Sandra to announce that she had won a big surprise gift from the Ellen show, and no they were not police officers, but Ellen's employees in disguise.

Jim shifted more in his chair. "The investigation is ongoing ma'am, it takes a while to go through every piece of the puzzle. The people in the news business move on to other 'hot' items, but our process is slower . . . but steady."

"Okay," she said, the excitement in her eyes undiminished. Sandra noticed a half-smile at the side of her mouth.

"What do you want to know?" the woman asked casually.

"Why don't you start with what you remember about the day. Let's start a little after you woke up," Jim replied.

The woman said that she would have no problem recounting the day at all. From the moment they learned about Sara's disappearance, she and her husband had re-lived that day many times, searching their memories and trying to recall whether they had seen her in any of the stores, or the coffee shop, or just on the sidewalk. But to no avail.

"What time did you leave the shopping center?" Sandra finally spoke.

"My husband thinks somewhere around 3 PM but I think it was around 4 PM, maybe slightly earlier." The woman leaned back on the recliner and broke out laughing.

Jim and Sandra looked at each other, unsure about what was so funny.

"You might be wondering . . ." She wiped her eyes with a Kleenex and continued, "My husband was not in the greatest mood that day. He was complaining about having to stand in all these stores while I shopped. The last store we went to was New Marine. I was mostly shopping for ladies stuff . . . bra, panties, you get the idea. He didn't want to tag along behind me. Being surrounded by women's undergarments made him uncomfortable, he told me. That's a bunch of garbage if you ask me. The old man cannot get enough of them at home, no matter what size. Sniffs them like a dog. But when you shop for it . . ."

She gave another hearty laugh and wiped her eyes with a Kleenex. "We were in that store for a while. I like to try my bras on before buying and they had only one changing room available. It was quite a wait, more so for my husband. When I finally emerged from the pay counter holding my shopping bags, he was standing near the entrance. As soon as I saw the look on his face, I knew it was the last of the shopping for the day. He was done. He saw me coming toward him, but he turned around and bolted. I struggled to get out carrying all the bags. I noticed he was already sitting in the front passenger seat. It was my car that we took that day . . . registered under his name but my car. He never drives my car, another 'woman' thing I suppose." The woman rolled her eyes. Their brightness never diminished.

"I opened the trunk and tossed in my shopping bags. I sat behind the steering wheel and then backed up my car. He said nothing, just looked out the window. Thinking, I guess. I gave him something else to think about. I told him one day in almost a year he comes along with me to shop and he still finds a way to upset me. If not, why make a big issue out of this? If you come to shop, you walk around, you stand, you do whatever it takes, because your wife has given you so much . . ." She continued, "I gave him a lot of shit like that to think about and I was probably getting louder and louder by the second, too. He didn't say anything at first. I was driving toward the main Greenmile Walk shopping area. The NEW MARINE is outside of the main section, you know?" She looked at Jim and Sandra to see if they understood what she meant.

Both Jim and Sandra nodded.

"Okay. So, I am in this narrow road that connects the New Marine side of the shopping center to the main section of the shopping center when suddenly my car skids. I tried to balance it by turning the steering wheel this way or that way. I floored the brake but somehow felt like the brake had already been applied. That was because my scumbag husband had pulled the engine brake all of a sudden." She shook her head and continued, "At first I didn't realize what had happened. My heart was beating fast and my body was shaking so much. When I looked at him, all I saw was his hand on the engine brake. I presumed he had pulled that to gain control of the car, like I was trying to by flooring the foot brake. Only when he started to yell at me for being a bitch and for ruining his life did I understood what had happened. He yelled in a fury; I matched him with equal fervor. That went on for some time. I heard a lot of honking behind us and eventually people passed through the other lane, all the while flipping their middle finger." There was another big laugh. Something moved vigorously inside her throat every time she laughed.

"It all seems funny now, but oh we were fucking furious when it was happening in real time."

"How long did you guys . . . actually, forget that . . . how long were you stopped in that spot before you moved again?" Jim asked.

"Umm . . . I don't know. It felt like eternity. I was crying at one point, too and just sat there. I then wiped my tears and drove again. People were getting pissed behind us. Wouldn't be able to tell you exactly how long we were there."

"Did you notice anything other than people honking at you and flipping you the middle finger?" asked Jim.

"I don't think so. Fighting, car horn, screaming drivers, I don't think my brain had any capacity left to notice anything else."

"When you were arguing with your husband, did you have your windows open?" Sandra asked.

"What?" For the first time during the conversation, the woman looked confused, unsure. But that uncertainty quickly vanished. "Yeah . . . like I told you earlier," she grunted back.

No, you didn't.

What followed was a long silence. Jim was busy writing on his notepad as fast as he could. Sandra was staring at the woman. The woman welcomed the challenge and reciprocated. After he was done writing, Jim raised his head up and said, "Ma'am, thank you for your cooperation. That concludes our questions for now. I would like to have a chat with your husband as well." Jim took out his business card and handed it to the woman. "Please have him call my cell phone, as soon as he gets back."

The woman took the business card and studied it.

"If you remember anything that we missed discussing, let us know. Remember, nothing is insignificant to us. However minor the recollection may be, let us know." With that Jim shook the woman's hand and headed out to the front porch. Sandra was already out on the porch, fiddling with a cigarette.

FIFTY-SEVEN

December 2016

andra looked at her phone again. *35 Elm Street . . .* Something clicked in her mind. She closed her messaging app and pressed the dial icon on her iPhone. "Hey Maggie, it's Sandy . . ." She waited for a moment. "Un-huh . . . yeah, came home early today. How are you?" She listened for a minute. "Un-huh . . . I understand, crazy huh! Hey, listen, can you do me a. . ." She paused.

After a brief silence, she said, "Yeah . . . I am still here. You know what, I was going to ask you to see if Jim was around. He wasn't picking up my phone. But I found what I was looking for, so never mind. Thanks though! Talk to you tomorrow . . . yeah . . . bye!"

No, she wasn't going to ask about Jim. But rather if she could grab her notebook from the Sara Sardana case. But just in time, she remembered that Jim would still be there, and she didn't want to alert him. At least, not yet. She had a better idea. She opened her Chromebook and typed *35 Elm*

Street, East Hampton, CT. The first result was from Google Maps. She clicked on the map, and then went to Street View. That was the street. She dragged the picture on the screen and rotated it so that she could see the house.

That was the dilapidated house that they'd gone to inquire about the stopped car. *Rose*, the name came to her. That was the woman who had answered the door. A little movie played in her head about her and Jim's visit. She could see the house, the door, the woman, the living room. Now, Sandra could also see what had bothered her. "Come on in," Rose had said with a broad smile when Jim had asked if they could talk to her. No complaining, no surprise, no, "What is this about?" Just "Come on in," as if . . .

At one point, she had held Jim's hand. Sandra couldn't visualize what they were talking about, but she could clearly see Rose's hand on top of Jim's. Then there was the story. Yes, the story. Too perfect? Too rehearsed? As if . . . as if Rose had expected the knock on the door. A police's knock on the door. She was prepared.

Sandra looked at the time on her phone. 5:35 PM. 35 Elm Street would be 20 minutes away from her home. She asked herself, what did she really know? Facts?

> *The car stopped. Created the traffic pattern. Fact.*
> *It was Rose's car. Fact.*
> *Sara was last seen walking in the direction where the car stopped. Fact.*
> *Sara climbed inside the stopped car. Not sure.*
> *Arun did not know anything about the driver of the stopped car. They'd only told Arun that the stopped car hypothesis was a dead end. Fact.*
> *Arun had independently identified Rose as a child abuser and wanted police to investigate. Fact.*
> *Arun had no idea about Rose and her potential connection to Sara's disappearance. Fact.*
> *Rose had never mentioned a child who lived in the house. They had asked if she had children and she had said no. Fact.*

Then she asked herself, what did her intuition say?

> *Rose was too nice.*
> *Rose anticipated a police visit.*

She had rehearsed the story.
She was hiding something.

Sandra looked at the time again. It was 5:40 PM. She pushed to her feet, grabbed her service weapon, her badge, and left her apartment.

FIFTY-EIGHT

Ms. Galligar. Hi, Sandra Moynihan from the Worcester Police Department. We met before!"

"Oh! Hi." Rose extended the "i" extra-long and offered her hand to Sandra. "Sorry, I am a mess. Just got out of the shower. I hope you didn't have to wait too long."

Sandra shook Rose's hand.

"What is this about?" Rose inquired with a frown.

"Someone filed a complaint in our department regarding endangerment of a minor. I am looking for . . ." Sandra pulled a case document from another case and pretended to read it, "Gabriel?"

Rose's cheerful face was gone, substituted by a blank stare. "Who complained?" she asked sternly.

Now that is more like you, Rose! Nice, drop the facade! It is so good to finally meet you.

"I can't disclose the source, ma'am." Sandra matched Rose's blank face and continued, "Does Gabriel live here?"

"Yes," Rose answered.

"We didn't talk about him last time . . ." Sandra asked.

"You didn't ask last time," Rose shot back.

Sandra looked displeased and said, "Umm . . . I am pretty sure we asked you if you had any kids."

"I remember what you asked. You . . . rather your partner asked if we have any kids. I told him we didn't have any kids. Gabriel is my grandchild, my dead daughter's kid, not mine," Rose answered sternly.

"I am sorry, Rose . . . I didn't . . ."

Rose raised her hand and said, "Save it officer. Just tell me what you need?"

This is more like you, Rose!

"I need to see Gabriel," Sandra replied.

"He is sleeping in his room. I am afraid I don't want to wake him up." Rose answered.

"That's fine. I can go look where he is," Sandra replied.

Rose folded her arms and gave Sandra a disgusted look. Rose turned around and walked inside; Sandra followed. Their living room was to the right, eat-in-kitchen to the left, and Sandra saw that the hallway led to three more doors. One straight ahead at the end and two on the opposite sides of the wall. Rose opened the door straight at the end, turned the lights on, and stood in the room with folded arms. Sandra stepped inside the room and saw a bald kid sleeping in a hospital-like bed.

She turned to Rose and said, "I will have to check for bruises on his body. I will try not to wake him up but I cannot promise."

Rose didn't say anything, she just looked at her grandchild. Sandra of course was making all this up. She didn't have any authority to do this. There was no official report filed. But she felt very strongly that she would find something in this house. Something was amiss. She went over to Gabriel's bed and removed his blanket. He was wearing his nightdress. Sandra thought it was early for bedtime. She looked at his legs, arms, back, chest, and buttocks for signs of physical abuse but didn't find any. He was amazingly cooperative, didn't wake up at all despite Sandra moving him every which way. She checked his pulse to make sure he was still alive. He was.

Disappointed, she pulled the comforter up and turned to Rose. "All set," she said and walked out of the room.

Now what?

In the hallway, she saw that the door on the right was flung open. It was a bedroom. The door on the left was closed. Through the small opening between the bottom rail and the threshold, Sandra could see that the room was well lit. She turned back around and said, "What's in there?"

FIFTY-NINE

Arun first heard the sound of the floorboards creaking outside the room, followed by the boot steps. The sound of the boot steps moved closer to the room, passed the room, and then stopped. He heard murmurs but nothing coherent. After several minutes, he heard the floorboards creaking again and then the boot steps. They stopped. This time right outside the room. He clearly heard, "What's in there?"

Arun jerked. *Sandra!*

Arun felt the increasing pressure on his face. Everything was dark because of the pillow covering his face, but suddenly the pressure was gone as well as the darkness. Gary had removed the pillow from Arun's face and put it on Arun's lap. Gary put his index finger on his lips and looked at Arun with wide eyes. Sweat trickled down Gary's forehead into his eyes. He turned around and looked at Sara to make sure she understood as well.

Arun glanced at Sara and saw something different. For the first time, she didn't have a blank face, or a sad face. He saw . . . hope! He felt hope too. But that hope turned out to be extremely ephemeral, as they witnessed Gary's next move. Gary pointed the gun directly at the closed door. Arun understood what that meant. If Sandra opened the door . . . *BANG!* She wouldn't even know what hit her. A similar fate would probably await him and Sara as well, Arun thought. He considered screaming and rattling the bed to get Sandra's attention. He didn't care if he died. He didn't have much reason to live anyway. His career was over, his personal life in the trash, and he had no other motivation to live. At least Sara would live.

Arun considered attracting Sandra's attention and ran all likely outcomes in his head. He concluded there was only a slim chance that both Sandra and Sara would survive the encounter. He decided against rattling the bed.

SIXTY

Rose had turned the lights off in Gabriel's room and was about to close the door. When she heard Sandra's question, she shut the door with a bang, took the towel off of her hair, and stepped forward. Her nose was almost touching Sandra's. "You listen to me, Officer. I have been more than cooperative with you. You needed to see Gabriel and I let you. I now ask you to step outside of my house and go away. If you need to ask any more questions, you will need to talk to my lawyer. I have had enough."

Bingo. Whatever you are hiding, it is in there.
Sandra assessed the situation. She could open the door and it could

be locked. If that was the case, Rose wasn't going to open it. It could be unlocked, and she might find something, but what? Gabriel was fine, she'd just checked. Had Sara really gotten in the car with Rose? But why? Sara didn't know Rose, so there would have been no reason for her to do this. Besides, the voicemail indicated that she had gotten in the car with someone she knew well.

Or it could be a bust like Gabriel. If it were a bust, then she would be in big trouble. There was no child endangerment report, and she didn't have a search warrant. She would not only lose her job but could face other serious repercussions as well. Maybe no jail time, but this would be serious. Risk outweighed reward.

Sandra gave a quick nod to Rose and said, "Very well then! Goodnight, Ms. Galligar."

Rose didn't say anything. Sandra walked out.

Rose stood at the door and watched Sandra walk over to her car. Rose didn't like this one bit. This cop woman was suspicious and that couldn't be good. She had almost opened the door, and would have if it hadn't been for Rose's quick thinking. If she came back with a search warrant, game over for Rose. She had to do something. Something quick. She reached for Gary's hunting rifle hanging behind the front door.

Whatever you are hiding, it's in there.

On her way to her car, which was parked on the other side of the road, Sandra considered how to get inside that room. She needed a search warrant but based on what they had so far, the Worcester County D.A. would not give her a warrant. Even if Sandra were to put a well-done steak in front of the D.A., she would ask Sandra to cut it for her and put it in her mouth. Rose's case was medium rare at best. No chance.

She put her car key in the ignition, but before she could turn it on, *BANG!*

SIXTY-ONE

S ara heard the boot steps fade away. She closed her eyes and slumped her head. Her hands were still tied to the bed rails. Gary stopped pointing his gun at the door and got behind Sara. He rubbed his jeans against Sara's buttocks. "OOO . . . That was fucking scary huh!" Gary said, drooling over Sara's buttocks. "I am fucking glad that's over. Now let's get to the business, shall we?" He kicked his boots off, pulled off his t-shirt, and pulled his jeans down. He pressed his crotch against Sara's buttocks and rolled his hand in front to cup her breasts. He let out a silent moan. He kneaded Sara's breast and rubbed his limp dick on Sara's buttocks. Sara knew what was coming next. Gary always did this before he raped her.

Gary's hands slid down from her breast slowly to her hips. She now felt his breath on her back. Sara cringed, closed her eyes, and buried her head between her breasts. Gary spread her cheeks and *DEEP BREATH!* He buried his nose deeper and *DEEP BREATH! DEEP BREATH!*

She was still cringing when her eyes suddenly opened. She was looking down at the foot of the bed where Arun lay motionless, stunned.

Gary took a last *DEEP BREATH!* Then he stood up, now hard and ready. Sara turned around. Gary looked at her as if he had seen a ghost. She had never looked at him like that. He saw big brown eyes, a pale face. In movies, he had seen old dead whores turning their heads completely backward. He soon realized this was all in his head when Sara bit her lips and said something. He didn't hear at first. She said it again, "In my mouth."

Gary grinned ear to ear. Sara was looking at her cuff. She shook her hand, metal clanked softly. Gary understood what she meant. He turned around with excitement and looked for his pants. He found the keys and opened her right cuff. He couldn't get his eyes off her lips. They were moist. All this time, Gary had found her lips dry and purple. And now, they were bright pink, wet and juicy. She grabbed his dick and gently stroked.

Gary just stood stunned. Sara had never shown any interest in him. She was finally liking it, he thought. It was going to be more fun now. So far it had been like fucking a dead cow. Now it would be fun. He loved the way Sara was touching him. Sara bent her knees and squatted. One hand on Gary's dick and the other still cuffed to Arun's bed.

Sara licked Gary's dick. He moaned. She put it in her mouth and rocked slowly. Gary stood akimbo, his head slowly turning up toward the ceiling. When Sara gagged herself, he was completely facing the ceiling. His eyes were closed, his mouth was uttering inaudible sounds of pleasure.

Sara continued to gag herself. He was still facing up at the ceiling when Sara suddenly took his dick out of her mouth. He felt something cold between his balls. He opened his eyes. His brain told him *ICE . . . that bitch is good . . . But where the fu . . .* Before he could complete his thoughts, *BANG!*

SIXTY-TWO

Sandra was about to turn the engine on when she heard, *BANG!* She looked over at Rose's house. She saw Rose turn around and run inside the house with something in her hand. Sandra got out of the car and ran behind her.

Gary felt numb, then a sharp pain. He screamed with all his might. He looked at Sara and saw a gun in her hand. He must have dropped the gun on the bed when he walked behind Sara. *Fucking bitch!*

Sara was bent to her left. She was covering her left ear with her left arm and her right ear with her right hand, which was still holding Gary's gun. Her ears were ringing painfully. In the heat of the moment, she hadn't realized how close she was to the gun. She couldn't hear anything other than the ringing in her ears. She looked at Gary, his mouth was moving violently. The wall behind him was a red mural.

The door flew open. Sara saw Gary's eyes move toward the door. He was moving his mouth with more vigor. She stood up, raised her hand, pointed the gun at the door.

BANG!

A single shot entered Rose's frontal lobe. Unlike Gary, Rose did not move her mouth or her eyes. In less than two seconds, she lay slumped on the floor. Parts of her brain were plastered to the wall behind her. Gary's hunting rifle dropped on the floor.

SIXTY-THREE

When Sandra reached the front door, she heard another *BANG!* Right in front of her eyes, Rose slumped on the floor. *WHAT THE FUCK!*

Sandra reached for her service gun and pointed it at the door, where Rose now lay motionless. She walked slowly and cried, "Police. Hold your fire. This is the police, hold your fire."

Sandra didn't hear any more gunshots. She could hear a loud wail. A man's cry. He was screaming, wailing and cursing, "FUCKING BITCH . . . GODDAM BITCH . . ."

As she reached the door she saw Gary with his back on the wall, wailing in pain. The wall was painted in his blood. She still did not see the shooter. Slowly, she saw the foot of a bed, then a naked woman with her hands over her face, her body drenched in blood, and a gun in her right hand. Then Sandra saw another body on the bed, this time a naked man, with hand and head cuffed to the bed.

"DROP YOUR GUN," Sandra screamed.

Sara didn't move.

"DROP YOUR GUN NOW . . . "

Arun was helpless. He could hear Sandra instructing Sara to drop the gun, but he couldn't do anything beyond moving his eyes all over the room. He strained his eyes all the way to his left, but he still couldn't see Sandra. He wanted to tell her that Sara was harmless. She'd only fired at her captors. *Please don't shoot. You will kill a victim. Please don't shoot, Sandra, Sara is innocent. Sara is harmless . . . harmless to you.* But he didn't move. He didn't know if that would alarm Sara, which in turn would alarm Sandra. He didn't want to startle either of them.

"DROP YOUR FUCKING GUN," Sandra said again.

The gun slipped out of Sara's hand and dropped on Arun's naked legs. Arun breathed a sigh of relief. It was over. Sara lived. Sandra lived. He was surprised, even he lived.

M.K. Shivakoti

PART THREE

SIXTY-FOUR

Ten months later

Arun unlocked his phone and opened the notes app. *430 Lakeview Drive.* A white cab stopped, and the driver waved in his direction. Arun pulled his carry-on and walked toward the cab. The driver put Arun's carry-on in the truck and soon afterwards, they left O'Hare.

It was a nice autumn morning in Chicago. Although Chicago fall couldn't match New England's, it was still fall. Misty and foggy with colorful trees, the city looked dreamy, beautiful.

After several minutes, the cab stopped. Arun added five dollars' tip, paid the fare, and climbed out. He took his luggage out of the trunk, and the cab left right away. Behind Arun was a tall apartment building. He climbed a few steps and opened the glass door. There were mailboxes on one end of the wall and buttons with numbers on the other end. He went to the end with buttons and pressed the button next to number 24. "Who is it?" Arun heard a woman on the other end.

After a brief silence, he pressed the button again and said, "It's me."

"Who?"

"It's Arun."

He didn't hear anything. Half-a-minute later, the door buzzed. Arun opened the door and jumped in the elevator. Inside, he pressed another button that was next to 2. He got out of the elevator and followed a hallway sign that pointed 21-24 to the right. Apartment 24 was at the end of the hallway. In front of the apartment door was a red mat that read "Welcome." *How ironic*, Arun thought. He knocked.

He immediately heard someone running toward the door. Arun smiled. The door jerked open but stopped after crashing into the door guard. He saw tiny eyes peek through the two-inch gap between the door and the jamb. Then he heard the most amazing sound in the world, "BABA!!"

Sunny exclaimed, "MAMA, it's BABA!!" He jumped up and down and kept banging on the door. Arun heard more footsteps inside the apartment. The door closed briefly and opened again, this time ajar. Arun saw his wife. She was standing right in front of him, blocking everything behind her. Arun couldn't tell if she was looking at him with disgust or indifference. Before they could say anything to each other, Sunny squeezed past his mama's legs and came right into Arun's arms. Arun finally understood why he'd wanted to come to Chicago. Sunny gave him a big tight hug and kissed him on his right cheek. Arun reciprocated Sunny's hug and kissed him on the neck. Sunny's cheeks were glowing cheerfully, unlike Arun's, which were now wet.

Sunny's expression abruptly changed. He turned his head around, looked at his mama, turned back to Arun and said, "It is okay, Baba, we won't leave you again."

Ashley gave up guarding the door and went inside the apartment, the door still only ajar. Arun put Sunny on the carpet outside the apartment. Sunny pushed the door wide open, held Arun by his fingers, and pulled him inside.

Ashley's apartment was similar to what she and Arun had back in Worcester. The front door opened to the living room, a small dining space was to the right of the entry door, and the kitchen was farther to the right. Arun assumed the bathroom and bedrooms were somewhere at the back. Before Arun had left for Chicago that morning, he had stood exactly in this same position outside his apartment door and wondered what he was doing. He had gone back inside to double check if he had turned off the gas knob. That wasn't necessary; he hadn't turned it on in months. Creature of habit, perhaps. As he was coming outside, he had noticed a brown package on the dining table, along with other pieces of mail. He'd picked up the brown package and looked at the sender's address one more time. Not that he needed to; he had done exactly the same thing earlier when he had seen it in the mailbox. He'd hesitated for a minute, then opened his carry-on and put the brown package inside. He'd locked the entry door and headed to the airport.

Since he wasn't being asked to sit yet, Arun just stood and looked around. He felt a pull on his finger again and Sunny took him to the middle of the living room. Sunny's toys were all over the carpet, including his Paw Patrol figurines and the lookout. Sunny jabbed at a small space on the carpet, untouched by his toys. Arun understood and duly obliged. Sunny started to talk about his figurines, what they were up to these days, his new favorite toys, and did Arun know that Anthony was his best friend in Chicago? Arun smiled. His left hand rested on the carpet, balancing his upper body, and with his right hand Arun played with Sunny's hair.

"What happened to your mouth, baba?" Sunny asked furrowing his brow, gently touching Arun's lips.

Arun smiled. "Just a little boo-boo, but it's getting better now. Don't you worry, okay?"

Sunny nodded and went back to playing with his toys.

Arun looked up at Ashley, who was now sitting in a chair in the dining area.

He got up and walked over to get his luggage inside the apartment. He took out the brown package. He put the package on the dining table and said, "I didn't want to impose but I had promised this to you."

"What is this, Baba?" Sunny said with a twinkle in his eyes. Arun hadn't realized that Sunny had followed him to the dining area. "Mama, surprise gift?" He looked at Ashley. She looked at him and smiled. It looked forced.

"Open it," Sunny said.

She didn't protest. With one swift motion, she ripped the package open and pulled out what was inside—a book. A post-it note covered part of the title. The handwritten note read, "First copy." Ashley took out the post-it note, and the title was now in full view, *Finding Sara Sardana*. Sunny snatched the book from her hands and ran toward the living room.

"I cannot accept this," Ashley said.

"I promised I would give you the first copy if I ever finished a book."

"You promised a lot of things, Arun."

"But . . ."

Ashley turned her head and looked outside the window.

"At least tell me that you're coming back to Connecticut," Arun said.

"I'm not."

"Why not?"

"I have a better position here."

"C'mon, Ashley! Sales strategy? Really? You fucking hate that sorta thing."

Ashley looked at Arun and raised her eyebrows.

Arun turned his head toward Sunny, who was in the living room, still flipping through the book.

"Sorry! But you hate corporate jobs," Arun pleaded looking back at Ashley and lowering his voice this time.

Ashley didn't say anything. They sat in silence for a long time.

Sunny came back after some time and said, "Can we go back to Hartford now?"

SIXTY-FIVE

It was a bright, sunny day, just like the day when Arun and Sara had gone to Six Flags. Arun got out of the car and walked inside the IHOP. The hostess asked, "How many?" He looked around for a familiar face. He saw someone. She waved. He waved back. He looked at the hostess and pointed in the direction of a young woman already sitting at a table. "Go ahead," the hostess said. Arun walked over to the table and sat across from the young woman.

"Hi Sandra," he said with a smile.

"How did it go in Chicago?" she asked.

"As well as it could have," he replied with a shrug. "We are moving on, Sandra. It is for the best. Best for Sunny," Arun added.

"He will be with Ashley then?" She asked.

"For now," He looked at Sandra. "Perhaps." He lowered his gaze.

"I'm sorry. I shouldn't have brought it up. I know it's hard on you, especially Sunny's situation," she said.

Arun didn't say anything.

A waitress broke their silence and asked something, but Arun was pensively staring at the table.

"Arun?" Sandra called.

He looked up at Sandra and then noticed a waitress looking at him curiously. She didn't say anything. He didn't understand.

"She is asking if you want anything to drink," Sandra clarified.

"Oh, just coffee please," Arun replied looking at the waitress.

"Cream and sugar?" the waitress asked.

"Just black please."

The waitress went away.

"So, why did you want to meet? The case is solved. I don't need to test your crazy theories anymore." Sandra grinned.

Arun looked up, unamused. Sandra threw her hands up. Arun smiled. "Not crazy, was it?"

Sandra shook her head, "Not at all. I thought I had seen it all."

"How is Jim taking all of this?" Arun asked.

Sandra smiled. "As well as possible. He has begrudgingly conceded that you played a part in solving this case. He says you got lucky though." She grinned.

"Lucky? Well, Jim should have been tied to the bed with his mouth stitched, and gotten raped by a crazy bitch. Then I would call him lucky." Arun shook his head.

"You know what he means. How you stumbled across Gabriel and all that," Sandra said.

Arun sipped his coffee.

"Did you ask Gabriel why he addressed Sara as Katie?" Sandra asked.

Arun smiled. "I don't think Gabriel knows Sara. He only knew Katie."

"You mean . . ."

"Yeah, Sara must have introduced herself as Katie to Gabriel . . . for all he knew, she was Katie."

"Why?" asked Sandra.

"That you will have to ask Sara," Arun replied.

Sandra frowned.

Arun took a sip of coffee again and said, "Although, I have a theory for that as well, but I am not sure if you want to hear yet another theory from this guy."

"Please! Entertain me. I have nothing better to do for the next hour." Sandra motioned her hand, instructing Arun to continue.

Arun obliged.

"Sara and I went to Six Flags once. She won a Styrofoam football in a ring toss, you know where you aim the ring to land over the mouth or the neck of the bottle?"

Sandra nodded.

"Well, she was ecstatic. She was showing it off to me and hurled the ball toward me. It landed on the floor, probably two feet in front of me."

Arun sipped more coffee.

"I laughed my ass off and told her *Kasto katie le jasto phaleko . . .* that's Nepalese for *You threw like a girl.*"

Arun looked for comprehension on Sandra's face. When he didn't see any, he said, "Katie is Nepalese for *a girl.*"

Sandra raised her brow and slowly bobbed her head up and down.

Arun continued, "Sara, of course, didn't understand Nepalese and I translated it for her, just like I did it for you. She laughed, laughed and laughed, and when she was done laughing she said, *'I am a Katie, you silly!'*"

Arun smiled. He sipped more coffee. "I don't know why she decided to just be a girl to Gabriel. You will have to ask her."

Sandra smiled and said, "I will."

There was a brief silence again. This time Arun spoke first.

"I am thinking about . . ." Arun paused, took a sip of coffee. "I am thinking about taking Gabriel's guardianship."

Sandra's eyes widened. She extended her hand across the table and held Arun's hand. "That's great, Arun!" she exclaimed. She pulled her hands back, her tone now turning somber. "You think you can do this?"

"I talked to my attorney and the state worker. They said we can sell his grandparents' assets, house, retirement account, etc. Half of that would go to Sara and half to Gabriel. All parties have agreed that Gabriel was a victim, too. The amount of Ketamine they put in him . . ." Arun shook his head. "I am worried what kind of effect that is going to have on him long term, you know?"

Sandra nodded. "We talked to doctors to find out if the use of

Ketamine explained Gabriel's, you know . . . talking to Katie and thinking it was a dream. But they thought there had to be something else too, such as mental manipulation, hypnosis, something else to mess up your ordinary sense of reality. Of course, only those dead fuckers would know what they did . . . but, yeah, all this is bound to have a long-term effect on him."

Arun nodded. He sipped more coffee and said, "Anyway, I can use the money to hire a home help for him. I think the state will help as well, but we will see . . ." Arun said. "I am taking him to Chicago."

Sandra raised her brows.

Arun continued, "That way, I can be closer to Sunny as well as take care of Gabriel."

"What are you going to do for work? Back to insurance, what was that, umm, Actuarial stuff?"

Arun smiled, took out a book from his laptop bag, and placed it on the table. "I think I will write. We will see how this is received. If well, then another one. If not, then maybe I'll freelance."

Sandra looked at the cover. It read, *Finding Sara Sardana.* She flipped the book open. The first page had just two words, *For Sara.* Sandra smiled. She looked up at Arun and asked, "Did you meet with her since . . . you know."

Arun shook his head. "My lawyer talked to her lawyer about the book, but that's it."

He looked outside the window. The day was still bright, the parking lot was full, but he wasn't looking at all. For a brief moment, a yearning flicked across his face. But it faded away quickly. He looked back at Sandra and said, "I can't."

She nodded. "Then you probably don't want to know how she got inside that crazy house either."

"She told you what happened?" Arun asked.

"Well. I am a cop, remember? When a victim is finally found, we have to take her statement. Besides, it's been all over the media. Have you been hibernating?"

Arun nodded.

"I am happy that she is alive and doing well . . . that's all I care about right now."

They finished their breakfast and went outside to the parking lot. "Thank you for meeting with me, Sandra. I just wanted to give you the book. That's all," Arun said.

Sandra stepped forward and gave him a hug. He hugged her back. Sandra turned around and walked over to her car. Arun was about to go to his car when he saw that Sandra had pivoted back toward him.

He waited.

"You were right about Rose and Gary," she said.

Arun looked confused. "Right about what?"

"That they were abusive . . . parents," she said.

Arun nodded. "I am just glad he is alive . . . the amount of drugs and manipulation . . . GOD!"

"Well, of course. There is that." Sandra paused, sighed, and said, "We were also able to ID his father."

Before Sandra could say more, Arun tuned out. It suddenly became apparent to him. How could he have not seen it before? Everything was right in front of him, wasn't it?

"She died two days later. Postpartum infection," Rose had said.

"Suicide . . . Rose was pretty devastated after her only child committed suicide . . . her daughter had refused skin to skin and breastfeeding. She apparently screamed to get the baby out of her sight . . . 'abomination' she had cried. Rose's daughter apparently kept saying, 'you could have stopped this.' . . . two days later, we found her daughter hung by the ceiling fan," the nurse at Worcester Memorial Hospital had said.

"He suffers from a birth defect, I think. He is blind because of that," Ann Horowitz had explained.

"It's just that I have wondered about her daughter as well . . . and Gary," the nurse at Worcester Memorial Hospital had said.

SIXTY-SIX

*December 2016 (A few days
after Sara was found)*

Michael Carter sat at the bar and put the newspaper on the bar top. He picked up the menu, flipped a couple of pages, and stopped at the page titled *Lunch Special.*

"Are you ready to order?" the server asked.

"Yes, red curry please!"

"Soup or salad?"

"Soup, please!"

"Which one?"

Michael looked at the menu again. "Hot and Spicy," he said.

Michael placed the menu into the outstretched hands of the server and rustled the newspaper to read the headline. ***Sara's Ordeal***, it read. Michael put his right hand inside his shoulder bag and took out his reading glasses.

On July 31st, Sara signed out for the day and hurried through the front door of Charming Lady. Earlier, she had seen the creep exit through the back door and wanted to make sure she would not have to deal with him again. She crossed the double lane road and went inside Amigo's Restaurant. Sam saw her coming in and waved. Sara smiled and waved back.

"Hey . . . got off early today?" Sam asked.

"Hi Sam! Yes, thank God! I didn't get a chance to eat my lunch yet . . . I am dying."

"I saw Christina earlier, why didn't you come with her?" asked Sam.

"I should have . . . well, can't do anything about that now . . . can I get my usual chicken bowl, please?"

"Sure, it will be right out," Sam said and handed her a paper cup. "Get something to drink . . . I will bring the bowl to your table. You can pay after you're done eating."

"Thanks, Sam!"

Sara finished her burrito bowl, paid, and stepped out of the burrito joint. She stood on the sidewalk and called Ross.

"Hey, I am done for the day, could you please pick me up?" Sara said.

Sara only heard slow breathing on the other end of the line. Then, "Could you take a Ride-O-Share today pleaseee! It's the fourth quarter and the Pats are trailing by two-points . . . please!"

"Sure can . . . no worries!" Sara said. "I will see you in a bit."

Ross sounded relieved. "Great! Thanks Hon . . . the game should be over soon, we can go out to eat if you would like?"

"Sounds good . . . but I just ate, maybe a little later?"

"Ok!" Ross said.

She hung up and opened the Ride-O-Share app on her phone. A circle appeared on the screen and an orange light moved around the circle in a loop. Sara waited a few minutes. Nothing. She pressed the home button and pressed the Ride-O-Share app again. The orange light was still circling around. With a sigh, she pressed the home button again and stuck her phone inside her purse.

She folded her arms and looked around. She wasn't sure what to do. She remembered Christina, her manager at the Charming Lady, mentioning a sale at the New Marine store. She looked at her watch, 3:37 PM. Sara thought she could shop for an hour and then go home. If Ride-O-Share still didn't work, she would call Ross again. By then his stupid game would be over. She hated Sundays. Ross sat on the couch all day watching every single game on TV.

She looked to the right, and immediately turned left and started walking toward New Marine.

Is it really him?

She glanced back over her shoulder.

God!

Michael Carter was coming out from *Baby Gap*, a little girl over his shoulder and another one walking and holding onto his pinky.

She picked up her pace. She wanted to get inside a store, behind a wall, anywhere but there. After a couple of minutes of walking, she heard someone calling out a name.

Shit!

She looked to her right.

A car stopped. The tinted window for the front passenger seat rolled down and a smiling woman greeted Sara.

"Hey . . . how are you? Katie, right?"

Sara was eating lunch by herself at the Mercy Hospital cafeteria when a voice said, "Hi."

She turned to her side, looked up, and saw a bald young man standing next to her, holding a white cane.

He said, "My name is Gabriel. I'm a boy. Who are you?"

Sara smiled. An old memory flashed in her mind. "And I am a Katie," she said merrily.

"Hi Katie. Can I sit next to you and eat my lunch?" Gabriel asked.

"Hi . . . I'm Sara. Katie was just . . . well, I'm Sara."

The woman looked taken aback, "I'm sorry, I thought you worked at Mercy Hospital few months back with my grandson Gabriel."

"I did . . . I know it's confusing. But my name is Sara."

The woman knitted her brows for a moment, brooding with a dark glare, but soon her expression eased. "Well . . . I'll tell Gabriel that we met Katie today . . . who is also Sara." She threw her head back and laughed.

Sara smiled.

"I'm Gabriel's grandmother."

"I know," Sara said. "I've seen you at the hospital."

"Where are you headed?" the woman asked.

What's her name?

"Well . . . I was going home from work. I work at one of the retail stores back there." Sara pointed to her right.

"I thought you found work in Hartford?" the woman asked.

Sara gave a dry smile. "Yeah . . . that didn't work out . . . For now, this is it."

She glanced over her shoulder again. Michael was walking toward her, but his attention was still on his girls.

"Well . . . too bad," the woman said.

"Is home that way?" the woman asked, pointing toward the New Marine.

Sara smiled again. "No, my phone is not working . . . I couldn't request a Ride-O-Share, so thought I would check out the sale at New Marine."

"Oh, we just got out of there . . . right, Gary?" She turned toward the man sitting behind the wheel.

He nodded.

"That place is a mess . . . too many people . . . stuff all over the floor . . ." the woman said.

"Really?"

"Not worth it. If you want, we could drop you home . . . don't you live in Worcester?" the woman asked.

"South Hampton . . . But you don't have to . . ." Sara said.

"Even better! We have to pass South Hampton on our way to East Hampton. Not a problem at all—we are heading home anyway. We will drop you home and then go home." Saying this, the woman reached for the door behind her and opened it.

Sara hesitated. She glanced back over her shoulder again. Both the little ones were now walking, holding onto Michael's fingers. He was looking directly toward Sara.

"Come on . . . quick . . . my husband is getting all the abuses in the world." The woman pointed to the cars honking and passing in the next lane. She threw her head back and laughed again.

Sara climbed inside the car and quickly closed the door. Soon the car was moving. Sara kept her eyes on Michael, until he could no longer be seen through the window.

She sighed and put on a seat belt.

"Oh . . . don't worry, my husband drives like an old man," the woman laughed again.

She turned around, twisting like a pretzel, and looked at Sara, "Gabriel would be so happy to see you, would you like to meet with him?"

"I . . . would love to . . . but I ha—"

The woman interrupted and said, "He talks about you all the time . . . poor Gabriel does not have many friends, you know!" Her bright smile was now gone. She dabbed the corner of her eyes with her index finger.

Sara sighed. "I would love to meet with him."

The woman's face brightened up. She reached out for Sara's hands, wiped her eyes, and looked at the man behind the wheel.

"Did you hear that, Gary? She will come with us," the woman said. Gary nodded.

"Do you know who she is?" the woman asked.

Gary shook his head.

"This is Katie . . . Gabriel's Katie," the woman said, widening her eyes.

"Mmm . . ." Gary said.

"Sorry . . . Sara, not Katie," the woman added quickly.

Gary raised his hat. "Pleased to meet you," he said with a Southern twang.

"Nice to meet you too," Sara said.

SIXTY-SEVEN

Gary parked the car in the driveway. He looked at his wife and said, "Rose, don't forget to grab your crap from the trunk . . . I ain't helping you."

Rose! That's her name.

Rose looked chagrined. She looked at Sara and said, "Please don't mind my husband's language. We have been shopping all day . . . well, I have been shopping all day and the poor guy has been standing the whole time . . ." She leaned over and whispered in Sara's ears, "Little cranky!" She threw her head back and laughed again.

They got out of the car. Sara helped Rose take her shopping bags inside the house.

Rose offered Sara a seat at the dining table. Gary went to the living room and turned the TV on.

Rose went to the living room and turned the TV off. Gary

complained. She looked at him sternly. He didn't say anything. He went over to the dining room and sat in a chair, across from Sara.

Rose looked at Sara and said, "Gabriel was asleep when we left . . . let me go check to see if he is awake now."

Rose went down the hallway. Sara raised the glass of water Rose had put in front of her and took a sip. She put the glass down and looked up at Gary. He was looking directly at her chest. She shifted her position. Gary continued to stare. Sara raised the glass of water and took a sip again. This time she didn't put it back down; she held the glass in front of her chest. Gary looked up and met her gaze; he looked away.

Something touched her left shoulder; Sara jumped. It was Rose's hand. Rose apologized for startling her. Sara smiled. Sara was about to ask about Gabriel when she felt a prick in the right crook of her neck.

"Ouch!" she cried and reached for the pricked skin with her left palm.

"I am so sorry . . . I must have poked you with my nail . . ." Rose said.

Sara turned to look at Rose again. Rose was grinning from ear to ear. Something was amiss.

"I think I should go now . . ." Sara said.

"But Gabriel—just a few more minutes, I will wake him up . . . Please, he will be so disappointed . . ." Rose said with concern in her eyes. Her expression suddenly changed, and she started laughing again. Sara looked at Gary . . . he was staring at her chest again.

Sara reached out for her purse and took out her cell phone. She pressed the home button, and the screen unlocked. She pressed the dial icon.

Rose tried to reach for Sara's phone. Sara pulled away. "Now why would you want to do that?" Rose declared.

Sara's head hurt. Something was not right. Sara tried to push Rose with her left hand. She looked at her phone again. Her contact list was on the screen. There was no time to think, she pressed the first contact on the list, *Arun Shah.*

Rose reached out and grabbed the mouthpiece. Sara tried to get hold of her phone. She struggled. Sara screamed for help. She cried Arun's name. She hoped he had picked up his phone. She cried. Her head hurt again, and the room spun. She lost her grip on the phone. Her hands crashed onto the dining table, sweeping the glass of water to the floor.

The last thing she heard before everything faded out was thunderous laughter.

SIXTY-EIGHT

Sara woke up. Her head still ached. She opened her eyes and saw a white ceiling. She blinked a few times and tried to get up, but she couldn't. Her hands were tied behind her head. She tried to move them; they only rattled. She looked down at her body and saw the horror. Socks were the only piece of clothing she had on. Something was all over her belly, it looked like dried saliva. The pain in her head had now shifted to her lower abdomen. She understood. Tears rolled down her cheeks. She screamed. She rattled the bed.

The door unlocked. Sara looked up. She couldn't see anyone. Slowly, Rose appeared on the right side of her field of vision; Rose was grinning. Gary moved past Rose and went over to the foot of the bed, he was drooling. Sara felt disgusted, vexed. She turned her head away from Gary and looked at Rose. Tears welled up in Sara's eyes. "Why?" she asked.

Rose smiled but her expression suddenly turned grim.

SLAP!

"Why?" Rose raised her eyebrows and leaned forward.

"Bitch . . . you ask me why?" Rose cried. "Did you hear that, Gary . . . this little bitch wants to know fucking why? Let me tell you why . . . Gabriel . . . that's why . . . you fucking bitch . . . you didn't have the decency to bid goodbye to that motherless child?"

Gary shifted a little.

"He was so happy and then you fucking bitch decided to leave without saying anything . . . you broke him . . . he couldn't do anything after you left . . . he became a fucking vegetable . . . and you ask fucking why? You should have paid for this a long time ago. I was going to find you and then fucking torture you. I had everything planned, you know. Your goddamn destruction, that is. But I couldn't locate your fucking ass. Now I understand why. I had been looking for Katie, when I should have been looking for Sara."

There was silence. Rose gave a half smile.

"And look now, the universe has sent you to me. I couldn't believe my luck when I saw you on the sidewalk. Now, you will have plenty of time to repent . . ." Rose said.

"Gabriel will be happy. He will see you every day now . . . he will be so happy again . . ." Tears rolled down Rose's cheeks. She wiped them away quickly and said, "If you tell him anything about what is going on . . . I will have no problem killing you. Remember, I killed my own daughter, hung her up by the ceiling fan. So, think about that before doing something stupid."

She paused for a few seconds and said, "Actually no, I won't kill you—that would be fucking easy. I am going to make sure you live—I am a nurse, you know—I am going to do everything to make sure you live . . . but you will live a tortured fucking life." Rose turned right and looked at Sara's naked lower body.

"How does your pussy feel today?"

Sara looked away from Rose.

"Well, that ain't nothing, bitch. That was just my husband inside of you. I am going to put so many things inside that little cunt, you will beg to die . . . You will beg to die, bitch!"

SLAP!

SLAP!

253

SLAP!

"So, make sure Gabriel knows nothing. He is going to think it's all a dream . . . I am going to make sure he will think it is all a dream. This will be his therapy . . . so that he can be sane again, so that he can talk to us and smile again, so that he can be happy again, like he used to be. You fucking bitch, talk to him normally—and don't you think we won't know what you say. See that thing over there?" Rose pointed to something behind Sara's head.

Sara strained her eyes and saw a black object up in the corner of the ceiling.

"That is a nanny cam," Rose continued, "We will know everything you say or don't say . . ." Rose bent down and pulled Sara's hair with her left hand, "You got that, bitch?" Rose let go of Sara's head and turned toward Gary, who was holding his crotch from outside his pants.

She grinned. "You want more, Hon?"

He bobbed his head and started panting.

"I want to see it . . ." Rose stepped back and grabbed a chair.

Sara closed her eyes and sobbed.

SIXTY-NINE

Rose and Gary brought Gabriel into Sara's room at night. Gabriel always seemed half asleep, half awake. Sara didn't know what they had done to him. But he always wanted to talk to Katie. Sara would reply as Katie. Then Gary and Rose would come back and take him away. He should know, she thought. He should know something isn't right. Why doesn't he know?

She had tried one time to talk to him as Sara, not Katie. She was mad. She couldn't understand why he kept talking to her everyday but didn't feel something was amiss. She was very mean to him that day. Gary and Rose had come in and injected something into his neck. Then Rose punched her. Sara was knocked out for two days. Later, Rose told her that she was happy about what had happened. Because of the incident, Gabriel didn't want to meet with Katie and Rose didn't have to drug him anymore. Rose said she was relieved.

Gabriel never came to Sara's room after that. She felt sad and helpless. Even if she had told him . . . what could he have done? For all she knew, these monsters would lock him up, too. Nobody else in the world cared about his existence . . . nobody would even look for him . . . But people knew her. How come they hadn't looked for her? She cried, she cried more . . . someone should look for her . . . Someone, please look for her . . .

SEVENTY

Michael Carter finished his lunch and signaled the waiter for the check. He folded the newspaper and put it in his shoulder bag. He looked up at the TV. Sara was everywhere. It was the breaking news of the year. Sara was found alive after five months in captivity. She had killed her captors and now waved to the crowd of reporters with a smile. Her boyfriend and her parents were by her side. She thanked everyone for keeping her in their prayers. She thanked the Worcester PD. She pointed to a lady officer who was standing behind her and said, "Thank you, Sandra." She wished Arun was here, she wouldn't be alive today if it weren't for him, she said. Detective Jim Kelly then took questions from the reporters.

A reporter asked Sara what she was going to do next. Sara said she was just happy to be alive and be with her family and loved ones. She hadn't given much thought to what was next.

The waiter brought a check for $15.43. Michael took out a twenty-dollar bill from his money clip and put it inside the check holder. Michael stood up, pushed the bar stool back, and grabbed his jacket from the back of the stool.

It was a cool day in Hartford. They'd had a snowstorm a few days ago and snow was still piled up along the side of the road. Michael passed through the snow dunes and went inside the gold building. He took the elevator to the fifth floor. He scanned his ID; the door opened, and he snaked through the maze of cubicles to his office. Michael could not shake Sara out of his mind. He thought about the conversation he'd had with Roman at the Marriott.

He was ruminating on these thoughts when he heard a knock on the door. "Come in," he said. Pam Knight entered.

"What's wrong, Mr. Carter? You look like you just saw a ghost," Pam teased.

Michael gave her a dry smile.

"Here are the couple of documents you asked for." Pam placed a folder on Michael's desk. "Did you hear about that South Hampton girl who was found two days ago?"

Michael nodded, without looking up. He was concentrating on the documents that Pam had just placed on his desk.

"I thought I had seen her before, you know?" Pam said.

Michael looked up.

"I had seen her in the news . . . but I didn't connect it, only when I saw her talk on that news conference, she seemed familiar . . . But I still can't place her exactly. Strange, isn't it?" Pam said.

Michael nodded and looked down at his desk.

After a brief silence, Pam said, "Maybe she was one of the girls we interviewed for Mr. Bland?"

Michael looked up again.

Fuck!

He gathered himself quickly and said, "I don't think so. She may just have everyday features."

"But—"

Michael interrupted and said, "I need to finish something before 3 PM this afternoon. Do you mind, Pam?"

"Of course! Of course!"

"And do you mind closing the door after you? Thanks, Pam!"

Michael said.

As soon as Pam closed the door, Michael booted up his laptop. He typed his password and opened a folder named *Bland Corporation*. He clicked on *Personal Secretary* folder and then *Accepted* folder. He clicked on the *Profile* folder. A window popped up with images of women wearing professional attire. He double clicked on each picture one by one. After he was done reviewing all 27 profiles, Michael went back to the *Personal Secretary* folder and clicked on *Rejected & Declined* folder. There were 413 pictures. Michael clicked on each, one by one. He stopped at picture number 410.

Sara.

Michael's heart skipped a beat. His meeting with her was protected by the NDA, but not what had happened at the Marriott. If she really wanted to go against Roman Bland, he wondered if the NDA would mean much anyway. An NDA was a smoke screen, a deterrent, so that the women they interviewed felt too afraid of the consequences to walk up to the police and complain. He wasn't worried about the ones who had accepted the job. They were aware of what they had signed up for. Besides, they would be on the losing end financially if they breached the contract, and Michael had enough documentation to prove that everything between Roman Bland and the women was consensual.

He was now worried about those who'd declined. If they breached the agreement, there would still be financial implications for these women. They still wouldn't be able to prove what Michael had said during an interview. The cards were stacked against any woman who would come forward. The only exception was if they ganged up. Normally that wouldn't happen either; there would be little to gain from coming forward. But this nice equilibrium was shaken up due to Sara's newly gained celebrity status. She now had a voice.

If she were to come forward and claim Roman had sexually harassed her at the Marriott, or worse raped her, and detailed her interview with Michael about a dubious personal secretary position, it would put Michael and Roman in an extremely precarious situation. They could still deny these allegations and of course she didn't have any proof. But her allegations could give the remaining 412 women reasons to come forward and support Sara. It would be impossible to look innocent if that many women accused them of the same thing. Sara's celebrity status, people's growing sympathy toward her, and other women corroborating her story would certainly leave Roman more than just vulnerable. This didn't look good to Michael.

He thought about calling Roman but decided against it. He needed a plan first. After staring at Sara's picture for more than twenty minutes and running multiple scenarios in his head, Michael finally decided. There was no other way. Everything they had done so far would blow up otherwise. Michael picked up his phone.

"Michael! What can I do for you?" Roman Bland spoke merrily on the other end of the line.

PLEASE DISAPPEAR

AUTHOR'S NOTE

THE INSPIRATION FOR THIS NOVEL came out of fear. My wife had called and asked me to pick her up from a mall. She didn't drive back then and had been shopping all day. It was Sunday evening and I was watching football when I got a call from her. I asked if she could share a ride instead. She didn't mind, and we finished our call pleasantly. But as soon as I hung up the phone, I felt tremendous guilt. This was during the early days of ride sharing and I hadn't been fully sold on the idea yet.

Nevertheless, I had suggested that she share a ride. What would I have done if something happened to her? Was football more important than my wife? How would I live with myself if she never came home? That and hundred other unsavory thoughts snarled me.

In the ten minutes that it took her to get home, I had already seen a nightmare. The seed for this novel was sown that day.

A year later when I started writing, I didn't know where the story was going at first, but soon different characters came out of nowhere and inserted themselves into the story. For the most part, I let them do what they wanted to do, I let them be who they wanted to be, but there were times when I intervened. If this story is flawed, that's because of my intervention.

If you would like to keep up-to-date with my latest releases, just sign up at https://mkshivakoti.com/contact-us/ and I'll let you know when I have a new book coming out. I would also love to hear your feedback about my book and any errors or omissions you may notice. You can email me at: contact@mkshivakoti.com

If you have time, I'd be really grateful if you'd be kind enough to post short review on Amazon or tell your friends about it. Reviews help new readers discover my book for the first time.

I love chatting to my readers, so please feel free to get in touch via:

Facebook page: Facebook.com/author.mkshivakoti,
Twitter: Twitter.com/mk_shivakoti
Goodreads: Goodreads.com/mk_shivakoti
Website: mkshivakoti.com

Thank you so much!

M.K. Shivakoti

ACKNOWLEDGEMENTS

I OWE SO MUCH to so many for their support and advice in writing this novel.

To my professors, Linda Tucker and Lynn Belcher, for drilling into my head that good writing is about being concise and clear. Although I am not always successful, I want you to know that's what I aim for.

To my beta readers and editors: Kristin Houlihan, Christine LePorte, Stephanie Diaz, and Megan Martin, for giving me your honest feedback and elevating my writing. This book is better because of your work. Thank you!

To my parents, Meena and Keshab Shivakoti, for loving and supporting me unconditionally. You let me navigate this world without much hand holding, giving me the opportunity to learn from my own mistakes. As a father, I am only beginning to understand how scary that must have been for you. I will forever be grateful.

To my brother, Saurav Shivakoti, for keeping me under your wings. I always felt secure and protected. I don't say this enough, but I love you man!

To my wife, Ruchie Bhattarai, for letting me sit in a corner and type away my imaginations. Every time I sit to write, I am taking your husband away from you. Thank you for your sacrifice. I love you.

To my son, Etash, for making me understand what love is. Only then I truly understood what fear is. It will be a while until you are old enough to read this book, but when you do, I hope I make you proud.

To my friends and supporters, thank you for accepting my work. As one author recently reminded me, the most difficult part about writing comes when one opens the office door and lets other people see the work. I'm truly blessed to have many encouraging and supporting people around me. Thank you!

ABOUT THE AUTHOR

BORN IN KATHMANDU, Nepal, M.K. Shivakoti came to the United States when he was nineteen. After working in the corporate world for almost a decade, he now writes full time. His interests are eclectic, but he is drawn to dark mystery/thrillers like a moth to the fire.

He is a strong proponent of diverse protagonists in commercial fiction.

He lives in Chicago with his beautiful wife and his son.

For more information, updates, and promotions, join his mailing list: https://mkshivakoti.com/contact-us/

Sample from

BLACK DOT, RED WATER

The Arun Shah Mysteries Book 2

Sara

My heart thumps in my chest as I walk toward the restaurant. Vito's is one of Hartford's finest restaurants, frequented by corporate denizens eager to utilize their privileged opportunity to expense their checks. I know I must be more than just assertive. I need to draw a clear line, before things get out of hand. Enough is enough.

I stop briefly to tie a loose shoelace, get up, and continue to walk toward the restaurant.

Someone could recognize me.

I shudder at the thought and pull the hoodie up.

After freeing myself, I've become a celebrity. I have to conceal myself from prying eyes whenever I'm out of the house. When I fail, half of those who recognize, pity; the other half, blame.

It's been more than a year since I killed Rose and Gary, and yet I cannot shake the feeling of not being completely free. I may be physically free, but the infinite world of thoughts, anxiety, fear, and worries still imprisons me.

Vito's appears ahead. I take my hands out of my sweatshirt's pockets and push the revolving door.

"Good evening! How can I help you?" a pretty brunette in a black business suit asks.

"I'm meeting with someone," I say as I search the floor packed with men and women in business attire.

A group of four middle-aged women sitting a few feet to my right look at me. They say something to each other and turn away. One of them picks up her wine glass and sips without taking her eyes off of me.

"What's the reservation under?" the brunette asks.

"Should be Michael Carter," I answer as I continue to search the floor.

"Here it is," the brunette says.

I still can't see Michael.

"Can I take your jacket?"

I hesitate but nod. Only when I begin to unzip my sweatshirt do I remember that I'm wearing an old T-shirt underneath.

"That's ok, I'll keep it on," I say.

The brunette nods. "This way, please!"

As we snake through fine people, sitting in fine leather, eating fine food, it doesn't take long to recognize Michael.

The back of his head gives it away. At first glance, it's like any other head in the restaurant—oblong shaped with professional looking short hair, slender neck rising like a stem from under the suit jacket. But in other inexplicable ways, it's like no other head. As we get closer to Michael's table, he turns toward us—beast smelling an approaching prey.

He smiles, puts his phone in his pocket and stands up. "Sara! Thanks for coming, please have a seat." He gestures with his open palm to the other end of the table.

Available on Amazon

Made in the USA
San Bernardino, CA
25 January 2020

63598416R00166